I0575129

MY DREAMS COME TRUE

MY DREAMS COME TRUE

AND OTHER DREADFUL TALES

ROCIO CARRANZA

QUEEN OF WANDS BOOKS
since 2024 | Austin, Texas
contact@queenofwandsbooks.com

My Dreams Come True is a work of fiction. Names, characters, places, and incidents either are the product of the author's imagination or are used fictitiously. Any resemblance to actual persons, living or dead, events or locales is entirely coincidental.
Copyright © 2025 by Rocio Carranza

All rights reserved. Published by Queen of Wands Books.

No part of this publication may be reproduced, distributed, or transmitted in any form or by any means, including photocopying, recording, or other electronic or mechanical methods, without the prior written permission of the publisher, except in the case of brief quotations embodied in critical reviews and certain other noncommercial uses permitted by copyright law.

Library of Congress Control Number: 2025919861
eBook ISBN 979-8-9921892-8-5
Paperback ISBN 979-8-9921892-9-2
Hardcover ISBN 979-8-9933391-0-8
www.rociocarranza.com

Cover Design by Rocio Carranza
Editing by Meg McIntyre, Phantom Pen Editorial
Interior Formatting by Rocio Carranza
Interior Illustrations by Amelia Mangham

First edition October 2025

Published in the United States

9 8 7 6 5 4 3 2 1

For all of you who watch rom-coms after a scary movie…
tell your sleep demon I said hi.

CONTENT WARNINGS

MY DREAMS COME TRUE IS A HORROR STORY COLLECTION. The stories within contain content that might be troubling to some readers, including but not limited to, depictions of and references to abuse, attempted sexual assault, blood, death, genocide, gore, animal death (single scene, non-explicit), manipulation, PTSD, strong use of language, and violence.

CONTENTS

AUTHOR'S NOTE

PART I

SLEEPY LITTLE TOWNS

Sleepy little towns are often quiet little towns,

much like peaceful little towns,

and happy little towns.

and in happy, little towns,

there are happy, little people,

with happy, little hobbies

that keep their bodies busy,

but none of those hobbies,

include the slashing,

and thrashing,

or smashing

of bodies,

because the bodies

of people

in *sleepy*,

quiet,

peaceful,

happy,

little towns…

THE SHED

November 18, 1982

Dear Nicole,

I am writing this in such a hurry.

I hope I can get the words on the page in a way that makes sense to you. I tried calling your landline, but I kept getting your answering machine…

I made it here yesterday. And yes, just like the doctor said, my father is acting quite strange lately. He's talking to himself, saying the most bizarre things. I wasn't able to sleep last night—I swear I can hear his voice through the walls of this damn house.

And today was horrible. He won't let me out of his sight. I only have time to write this because he's napping now. You were right, I never should have come back. But now that I'm here, I can't seem to get away from him. Please answer your phone, I need to hear your voice.

I have to go now, but I promise to write soon.

I miss you,
Margo

November 23, 1982

Dear Nicole,

Sorry I haven't been able to write much this past week—my father has been acting out. I received your letter two days ago in the mail. He tried to read it, saying he knew a Nicole. As if Nicole isn't a popular name. I tried to tell him the letter was mine, but then he started badgering me about why the Nicole he knows was sending letters to the house.

He kept saying, "That damn reporter will ruin everything!"

We got into a huge screaming match when I told him again that you were my Nicole, you're not even a reporter, and that I never heard of this other woman he was ranting about. Then he threatened to call my mother on me. He kept screaming *Sylvia! Sylvia!* as if she would've walked right into the kitchen then and there. As you can tell, it's getting worse.

I spoke to his doctor at his last appointment and they claim it's only a matter of time. I feel selfish, but I wanted to ask how much longer it will take. Being near him, being in this house is suffocating. But he's all alone.

I know you wrote that your answering machine

doesn't have any missed messages, but can you look again? I could've sworn I left you at least three. But if not, I'll try again later this afternoon and make sure to wait for the beep if you aren't able to answer. I can use a payphone if that helps, but I don't want my father to grow suspicious. He doesn't like deviating from his schedule, but I'll sneak out in the middle of the night if I have to.

I miss you. I hope we can talk soon. And please hug my cats for me, thank you again for keeping an eye on them.

Margo

November 30, 1982

Dear Nicole,
I don't even know how to explain this past week. Hell? Torture? The worst seven days of my life?

My father is out of his mind. Every single night he paces around his room, speaking to no one in whispers I can hear from down the hall. I don't even know how that's possible, but I swear I can.

I've confronted him about this a million times and he keeps claiming that I've gone insane. Me!

A few nights ago, I barged into his room and saw him

standing in front of the window. Just standing. I asked him if everything was fine and he said it was "now that the family is together."

What the hell does that even mean?

Now, I know the doctor says I shouldn't say anything to work him up, so I tried to hold my tongue. I told him maybe he needs a new prescription for his sleep meds, or to read a book, or something that would stop him from driving me completely and utterly insane in the middle of the night. But he kept telling me that it's my mother speaking to him. He was completely serious, staring at me like I had grown two heads when I tried to tell him she's not here anymore.
I shouldn't have done it, but I've slept barely six hours in the last three nights. Maybe all of this is making me insane.

He began screaming her name again, begging me to search the house for her. I felt horrible, but I didn't have the heart to tell him no.

We looked in all the rooms, under the bed, in the kitchen. All the while he was panicking and calling out her name. But when we passed by the window showing the backyard…Nicole, I swear the strangest thing happened.

He began to smile.

My father began to smile and waved out the window at the shed. "She's over there, honey. Look!"

I turned to where he was waving, but there was nothing there. It was just the shed. I've been making sure to double-lock the doors and windows, especially after what happened last time.

Please answer the phone. I miss hearing your voice.

Margo

December 2, 1982

Dear Nicole,
It felt so good to hear your voice today. Perhaps you're right, maybe my father's landline is having some issues. I'll be sure to call the phone company when I get the chance. In the meantime, at least we know the payphones are a good option.

I know I told you I would think about you coming to keep me company, and I really want you to. But with the way my father's been acting, I think you'd better stay home with Luna and Bastien. Give them extra treats for me.

I can't wait to hear your beautiful voice again and have

you in my arms. Hopefully soon.

Forever yours,
Margo

December 8, 1982

Dear Nicole,

I am so sorry I haven't called or written you back. My father has taken up nearly every bit of my time and sanity.

I'm happy to read that you're getting a promotion. It's about damn time they recognize what a wicked talent you are. I'm so proud of you, babe. I promise to take you out and celebrate when I get back.

As for your questions: no, I'm not sleeping well. I find myself nodding off during the day when I'm trying to clean the house or take care of this never-ending list of things to do. My father still makes noises at night, but they aren't whispers anymore. They don't sound like they used to. It's weird…

Last night, I tiptoed to his room and listened against the door. There were the strangest sounds, muffled as if someone was speaking far away. I'm not sure how to explain it exactly.

And then it was quiet.

I tried pushing my ear against the door, and I swear the second I did there was a huge bang. It was like something heavy fell on the floor. I immediately opened it, thinking the intruder came back for my father. But no. He was just standing there, looking out the window. He didn't even budge when I asked what happened. It was like he couldn't even hear me. Nothing in his room seemed broken—not a thing out of place. But I know I heard the bang. I know I'm not going crazy.

Nicole, I don't even recognize him anymore. It's like the man in this house isn't even my father. And this house...I feel like a ghost here. I'm starting to think that "a matter of time" may never come.

And I miss you, more than ever.

Margo

PS: I couldn't get a hold of the phone company, so I'll try to call when I can from a payphone.

PPS: Kiss the cats for me and tell them I love them. I hope they love me, too.

December 12, 1982

Nicole,

I'm leaving. I swear to god I am leaving once I find a nurse for my father. I can't stay in this house anymore.

My father is now sneaking out of the house in the middle of the damn night. It nearly scared me half to death. I thought the intruder had returned for sure. And all I could think about was how I shouldn't have come here. How I should've never answered the hospital's phone call. How I wished so badly to be with you.

When I finally got the courage to leave my room, every fucking light in the house was on. I ran into my father's room and he was gone. Completely gone. I freaked out and called his name. I ran through every room, thinking that someone had taken him or worse. Until I saw the back door wide open. And there was my father, standing in front of that shed.

Nicole, I want to come home. I want to be with you.

I love you,
Margo

PS: I've been calling, but it still goes to your answering machine. But at least I've been getting your letters. Please keep writing to me. You're the only thing keeping me sane.

December 15, 1982

Nicole,
I don't know what to say or how to start this letter.
So I guess I'll just get to the point.

The other day, I was washing dishes and noticed the
shed was slightly open. I think we both know that my
father had something to do with it. But it's weird, I
felt like I needed an excuse to go to it, and the door
being open felt like an invitation.

The shed is nothing remarkable. The wood is old and
gnarled, the red paint is dull now after being exposed
to the elements for too long. But with every step I
took toward it, it felt like the air around me thinned.
I know that sounds strange, but it's the only way I
know how to explain it.

I had this awful feeling in my stomach, like the kind
you get when the girl in the slasher flick is walking
down the dark road alone. You know something is
coming, but you don't know what it is. And that
feeling in your gut—in my gut—was telling me to go
back into the house.

But I needed to see what my father kept looking for.
Why was he so obsessed with this shed?

Nicole, I swear my hand was inches from the handle
when my father appeared in the corner of my eye.
Words cannot describe the fear I felt in that moment.
There is no possible way this sick man could have
snuck around me so fast. He was napping for god's
sake.
All he did was smile. That fucking smile. I can't close

my eyes without seeing it. I don't even know who he is anymore. This is not my father. This is ~~someone~~ something else entirely.

Why did I have to come back? Why was the funeral not enough? I will never do this to myself, to us, again. You are my family now and I love you.

Yes, Nicole, to answer your last letter, it was not a mistake writing those words.

I love you.

I love you, I love you, I love you. And when I come back, I promise to make sure you feel it every day of our lives.

Margo

PS: I'm still looking for nurses, but none of them are answering my calls right now. I promise, no matter what, I will be home by Christmas.

December 18, 1982

Nicole,
I know you say you're busy in the city and I guess it's true for people in the country, too. It seems no one is working in December. I've tried to call every nurse, doctor, and hospital in the area and it seems I can only reach answering machines or endless rings on the other end.

If I'm being frank, I still don't know why I haven't

been able to reach you by phone, Nicole. I know you're busy, and I am so happy for you.

But I need you. I need to hear your voice telling me everything will be okay…

I hate to say this, I hate myself for doing this, but I am leaving my father and going back home. I'll drive out on the 23rd so I can make it back in time for Christmas, like I promised you.

My father…he isn't my father anymore. I tried, I really did try, to talk to him about his behavior. The scratching at night, the whispers, the bangs, the shed, everything. But all he wanted to do was sit down and drink fucking coffee with a smile on his face. I told him that he needed to listen, to talk to me or I would leave, but he kept saying my mother wouldn't like that.

I lost it, Nicole. And for once, I'm not sorry. I screamed at him. I told him I was leaving in a week, told him that I couldn't handle being in this house with him anymore. I couldn't deal with who he's becoming. Then he became hysterical. He told me I couldn't leave, that we had to "be a family."

I stormed out of the kitchen as my father screamed after me. He's never done that before. And it wasn't his screaming that scared me, but what he said.

"She's waiting for you!"

Nicole, I'm writing this now with my door locked, still hearing the sounds from my father's room. I don't know why my father won't let her go—I don't know why he still pretends to talk with her. And I don't know why he keeps watching that fucking shed, but I'm starting to think that maybe there was no intruder after all…

Keep me in your thoughts. I love you.

Margo

December 19, 1982

Nicole,
I am going to the shed. I am giving my father his sleeping pills early so it will still be light out when I go. There's no way he'll be able to sneak up on me like last time.

I need to see what it is he's watching. Or what it is that he seems to want to keep hidden there.

Thank you for being so strong and taking care of things back home for me. Give my love to Luna and Bastien. But most of all, I give my love to you.

I love you, Nicole. You've always been my sweetheart.

Margo

PS: Once I see the mailman pick up this letter, I will go.

December 19th, 1982

Margo,
It's been over a week since I last got a letter from you. I swear, I have no missed messages on my answering machine. I had my dad come over to take a look just in case, but it's fine. I'm sure it's your father's landline, being out there in the middle of nowhere...

Luna and Bastien are doing fine. I decided to bring them over to my apartment since your stay at your father's has been taking so long. I hope that's okay.

Your last letter really worried me, and you should stay away from the shed. Please, even if it is nothing, it's not worth the risk.

I really think you need to come home as soon as you can.

Bring your father if you must, just come back safe.

I love you,

Nicole

PS: I can't wait to see you at Christmas. Luna and Bastien miss you.

Margo watched as the mailman dropped off and picked up the mail for the day. She thought about speaking to him, inquiring about the townspeople or whether there were any issues with the phones she should be aware of.

She put on her shoes and walked toward him, but he didn't seem to notice her, quickly tending to his business on the cold, windy day and jumping back into his truck.

"Wait!" she called out, picking up the pace. "I just have a question!"

Even as she waved her arms about, the mailman ignored her, shifting into gear and taking off past her house and down the dirt road.

"Asshole," she muttered under her breath.

A harsher breeze nearly pushed her back and she realized now that she was outside without a coat. She turned on her heel, looking at the house that didn't feel like her old home anymore.

Under a bleak, gray sky it loomed before her like a cage waiting to trap her. The vines that once grew along the exterior walls like a lush vertical garden now looked like claws grounding the structure in place. Promising, or threatening, rather, that the house would never let go. The wooden porch was rickety, in desperate need of repairs. The windows were nearly black so that she could not see through them even in the faint light of day. Perhaps that was the worst part.

Not knowing what exactly she was afraid of—that was always the worst part of being here.

Despite her nerves, she walked back inside and grabbed a jacket. She peered into her father's room and saw that the pills had done their job. Her father slept soundly, peacefully. He was snoring softly and Margo nearly forgot to be scared.

That is, until she heard it.

The sound of a door swinging open and closed outside. A faint, innocent sound, but one that brought Margo back to reality. She followed the sound, though she already knew what it was and where it was coming from. She walked back down the hall, took a right into the kitchen, and peered out the window just above the sink. The shed door was swinging open and closed, the wind pushing it just enough to reveal the darkness inside.

Margo swallowed and zipped her coat up to the top.

She felt numb, and not from the cold, as she stepped out the back door. She could hear the crunch of the snow beneath her boots, the sounds of the wind as it howled past her face. But her eyes were fixed on the shed.

Her imagination was working overtime, thinking up all the logical and illogical reasons the shed would be open and why her father was so fascinated with it.

She was closing in on it.

Her stomach twisted in knots she didn't know were possible, but her body couldn't stop moving forward.

There was something her father didn't yet want her to see…but the thing in the house was no longer her father, was it?

Her legs felt like she was trudging through quicksand, her heart thudding so loudly it nearly blocked out the sound of the wind.

And before she knew it, she was standing in front of the shed. The door was no longer swinging open, and the air was still and silent.

"Your mother's been waiting for you."

Margo didn't need to turn to know that the thing in her father's body was next to her. She couldn't respond, her lips trembling too much to form coherent words. Tears welled up in the corners of her eyes.

"Go inside, my dear."

Margo squeezed her eyes shut, but the rest of her body

betrayed her. It was as if she was no longer in control of herself as her hand gripped the handle.

She could run away.

She could jump in her truck and get out of Dodge in a matter of seconds if she just let go of the handle.

She could be with Nicole in the city, living together with her two cats in bliss.

"She wants to say hello." An icy, decaying hand placed itself on hers, forcing Margo to pull the handle.

"No," she whimpered, unable to stop, unable to run.

Together, they opened the shed door.

County News | Special Edition | 25/12/1982
THE CREST FALLS TRIBUNE

Christmas tragedy strikes Crest Falls community

BY NICOLE RENNER

A Crest Falls County man, 58, and his daughter, 32, were discovered dead in their home after an apparent murder-suicide, according to police. Detectives identified the two people as Michael and Margo Wallace, respectively.

Police found them unresponsive in a shed on Michael Wallace's property around 3:45 p.m. Friday after a friend of Margo Wallace requested police conduct a wellness check on the premises.

This is not the first tragedy to strike the Wallace home. Six months ago, Michael Wallace's wife, Sylvia Wallace, was the victim of an apparent home invasion turned murder. The suspect in that case has not been found as of this article.

Sheriff Gilbert Lewis of the Crest Falls County Sheriff's Department released the following statement: "Letters sent by Margo Wallace, obtained from a witness, indicate an ongoing conflict between her and her father, Mr. Wallace. It is the conclusion of this department that Margo Wallace was experiencing derangements that may have led her to tragically kill her father with sleeping pills before taking her own life with a weapon found on the scene. Due to these tragic circumstances, we are investigating the possibility of Margo Wallace's involvement in her mother, Sylvia Wallace's murder. We do not have enough information to disclose the status of our investigation at this time."

"You know damn well this was no murder-suicide, Lewis," Nicole Renner muttered to the sheriff. It was late, and they were alone at her desk as she typed the last words of the article set to run in next morning's print.

"I'm the one who found them. There's no doubt about it."

"Oh, so your word is gold, now?"

"Mine and the county coroner's, yes."

"Jeff can barely see two feet in front of him since his stroke. You should get a second opinion."

"It's the best we got, Nicole."

"Best my ass," she snapped as she eyed the open binder atop a cluster of papers on her desk. Nicole was never known for being neat and tidy, but the mess always made sense. She knew exactly where everything was. Just like she knew that this case was more than a daughter scorned.

"I don't know what to tell you—the facts are the facts. I'm sorry your theory didn't work out."

"The only fact here is that you're trying to clear your case load…the easy way." She snatched up the heavy binder and began to flip through the pages of clippings, statements, and crime scene photos. She lifted one of Sylvia in the shed, where she had been found in the same position as Margo.

"Bullshit, Nicole. You've been badgering Mr. Wallace for months and you got nothing. It's no surprise the man cut his phone lines."

"I'm a journalist, it's my job to uncover the truth." She waved the photo in his face. "And the truth here is that Michael's story didn't add up when his wife died."

"The man is nearly sixty for god's sake, you think he could've dragged his wife from the house to the shed without leaving a single shred of evidence?" Lewis threw his hands up and stood, clearly ready to end the conversation.

"All I am saying is that Michael was there the night Sylvia died, and he was there the day Margo died. If it is a murder-suicide, it's the other way around."

"We have a confession, dammit. The letters the girlfriend gave us clearly states that Margo gave her father sleeping pills. I don't know how much more clear cut it could be."

"Margo didn't write she was overdosing him, just that she was giving it to him early."

"Same thing." Lewis waved a noncommittal hand.

"And also, the dates are not lining up. The county coroner believes Margo died weeks ago—"

"The woman was going mad, Nicole. I don't know what else you want to hear. She could've mixed up the dates or something. I'm an investigator, not a mind reader."

"The letters she wrote to Nicole sounded quite sane to me."

"That doesn't prove anything."

"But—"

"The case is near closed and it's late. I'm going home before you keep me up all night with more of your crazy theories. Have a good night."

With that, Lewis left the room.

Nicole was alone now.

The single light above her desk flickered as it always did when she burnt the midnight oil.

She flipped through the photos once more.

Gruesome photo after gruesome photo filled the folder.

This was the twelfth mysterious death of its kind in the county over the past year. The others happened to families not so far away from the Wallaces. All were found in a shed. All were declared home invasions gone wrong or murder-suicides.

She finally closed the binder.

Maybe Lewis was right—perhaps she was concocting crazy theories.

Nicole pulled the pages from her typewriter and placed them in the editor's box for the morning review. She'd barely made it back to her desk when she heard a knock on the newsroom door.

Nicole looked up, startled, but it was only Lewis again. "Did you submit your article?" he asked as he leaned against the doorframe.

"Unfortunately," Nicole muttered as she grabbed her coat and purse. "Why are you back, did you forget your doughnut?" She scoffed.

Lewis smiled slowly, not taking the bait. "It's late. I thought I'd walk you to your car."

"Wow." She rolled her eyes. "It seems you finally learned how to be a gentleman."

She walked past him, fishing her car keys from her purse.

"It's a scary place out there," Lewis said. "If you want, I can drive you home."

QUEMAR

May 6, 1921

Dearest Deborah,

I had the most curious of days and have settled upon two facts I now know to be true.

First, I have recently mastered the inexplicable talent of entrepreneurship, a special intuition that favors only the finest of businessmen such as myself. I was on the eight o'clock train this morning to Pecos when I heard the most unfamiliar and welcoming voice from within.

Oil, it repeated, *oil*.

As we approached the next stop, certainly a great distance from our final destination, my senses urged me to remove myself from the train at once and venture into the land. And in the depths of my soul, I knew that an opportunity of the rarest kind had presented itself to me.

I dared not ignore it!

My associates followed me from the train and we set forth into a town they call Quemar. Mariano has procured the son of a local innkeeper to guide us further west into the vacant, desert lands tomorrow to see it for ourselves.

Second, despite its barren appearance, I am certain Quemar is rich with oil! The scorching heat boils the dirt with such intensity that, gazing upon it, I feared it may burst through at a moment's notice. I could feel the oil pulsing from within the tender earth, just beneath my fingertips!

If my intuition is correct, as I know it to be, I shall procure the appropriate paperwork to begin digging and acquire the land before word of it reaches my enemies. I will write again as time allows.

Ever your affectionate husband,
Albert Canterbury

ALBERT

Albert was not particularly fond of the West, nor did he much appreciate the heat. He sat up straighter in the train car and loosened his tie discreetly as his business associates slept, plagued as they were by boredom, or concentrated on their newspapers.

The knot wouldn't budge beneath his sweaty fingers, having been tied too tightly that morning in Albert's fit of rage amid yet another argument with his wife. He tugged at the fabric, cursing the damned thing.

He was fairly certain it had shrunk recently, as had his other clothing. One at time, in some way or another, everything around him shrunk. His pocketbooks, his influence, his ties to the east coast. And the smaller each became, the more he felt suffocated by it all.

With a final jerk, the knot gave way and he accidentally slammed his fist against the train window. A few eyes perked up, watching him. Albert coolly met their gazes until they slowly looked away.

Albert was an aristocrat from Boston who'd moved southwest in his prime, decades ago after attaining his business degree from Yale. Rumor had it that Albert's family had simply paid for the degree and he'd never actually stepped foot in a lecture, but such idle gossip never seemed to affect his success. Besides, he never cared to listen to the professors.

Albert sought to escape the miserable winter weather and expand his family riches elsewhere on his own merit. He took the last of his inheritance right from under his father's nose and scurried into the night like a rat in the city streets. After a few bouts of unlucky gambling and mounting debts, he went into hiding in the lawless land of Texas, where, with the last of his dwindling fortune, he'd struck black gold near Houston in 1902. The years that followed were good to the man. He invested in various successful   businesses moved about the state, was an occasional politician, served as the chair of numerous committees, and had his choice of women who were ripe for the picking—which he did, very often.

At his associates' urging to further bolster his public image, he settled down and married a local woman, Deborah Marsh, with the right familial connections.

As long as his pockets were filled and the numbers bore a plus sign on his profit sheet, he couldn't care less whether his refineries were too hot or if a man burned his hand clean off in the tank. Those were fools' mistakes, and mistakes that taught the rest of them a hearty lesson. They understood the risks and it was their decision to work. His only duty to them was to compensate them just enough—and barely enough—to keep any riots at bay. Albert was a fair man, not a kind man. And he saw nothing wrong with his methods.

It was something he told his wife after word of his illicit affairs reached her ears.

Oh, the embarrassment she felt having heard it from Mrs. Clara Withers during tea time while their children played in the adjoining room under the watchful eyes of their governesses. The shame of knowing that her fears were confirmed, wishing it could still be a kept secret.

Deborah understood that confronting Albert was a necessary duty, her part to play as a god-fearing wife of the firm belief that marriage was a monogamous venture. If she didn't confront him, then the next time Clara stopped by and inquired she would easily sniff them out and spread the town gossip that Debbie and Albert had an understanding. So, she did her duty and inquired, acting as erratic as any sensible, good woman would under the circumstances, only to be rebuked by her Albert, who was tired of the conversation as soon as it began.

"Debbie, my dear, have I not provided you with the luxuries of a well-kept woman? You need only say the word and my pocketbook would be happy to provide anything your heart desires, so long as you let me work diligently to make it so. Your tears only fall on the priceless jewels affixed to your delicate hands. I am fair, not kind," he had told her, silencing her for the time being.

The train to Pecos was a convenient, albeit arduous, mode of long-distance travel. And with numerous stops along the way, Albert would settle in for the days-long excursion by reading his books, the newspaper, or business ledgers. He seldom traveled alone, often accompanied by his longtime companions and business partners, Robert Perry and Mariano Ocampo, for protection. Even he understood that vigilante justice reigned in many parts of the southwest. A rich man alone was as good as a dead man.

Robert, a strait-laced Yankee from New York City, was middle-aged and stout with a large handlebar mustache that he stroked often while in deep thought. He did not come from a large fortune, but a moderate one which he'd inherited upon the untimely death of his parents in a fire. He did not speak often of the fire, but did speak about his adventures through the Bible Belt shortly after, where he'd tricked his current wife into marrying him by some secret means, gained property, and networked with her father's business associates. From there he worked as a co-owner in various trades until he met Albert, whom he convinced to make him a business partner by forging the signature of the notable entrepreneur Henry Walsh on a letter of recommendation.

To Robert's knowledge, Albert never discovered the trick, but considering it had been twelve years since, he'd long ago decided that it wouldn't change their partnership and ceased to concern himself with any form of guilt at the deception. Besides, he would assure himself whenever the memory resurfaced, they were far too successful now to part ways.

Mariano was a new addition to the group, having joined in the last three years. Particularly, in an effort to gain the sympathy vote of the working people during one of Albert's campaigns for political office. Albert's bid was unsuccessful, but Mariano's support did well for him in the long run.

He was a lawyer from Guadalajara who moved his family into Texas to escape the harrowing revolution under Carranza's regime. After offering his legal services to notable businesses throughout Texas, he successfully infiltrated Albert's posse with his wit and charisma. Mariano became an official member of his staff after successfully brokering a deal for land near San Antonio over a rival firm, Davenport Industries, which made Mariano a very rich man, too.

He was handsome, and the youngest of the trio at thirty-three; he was tall, with dark brown eyes and thick, black hair that he combed neatly into place every morning. Associating with Albert opened doors that he never thought possible, and he gladly took it upon himself to become the face of the people, even if it seemed he turned a blind eye to the wretched state under which the people labored.

But little did Albert know that guilt plagued Mariano. He'd recently sold business secrets to rival companies who promised better working conditions. It was only a matter of time before Albert would be forced out of the oil business, and Mariano's retribution would be paid.

On this particular trip, the three men sat in their private passenger carriage occupied by reading, writing, or sleeping, sometimes commenting on the growth of the towns from their windows as the train made its routine stops. Robert and Mariano spoke in hushed tones to better comfort the focused Albert, who did not care for idle talk.

Instead, Albert wrote a letter to his mistress—his most recent one, the wife of a wealthy land owner in Waco. So focused was he on the task that he barely heard the car attendant announce the train's upcoming stop in Quemar.

A forgettable stop. In all his years of taking the train through the Chihuahuan Desert of west Texas, Albert rarely saw anyone get off there. And never had he seen anyone get on. He was signing his name at the bottom of the letter when he heard a faint, almost inaudible whisper in his head.

Stop.

He peered over his newspaper at his partners, both sleeping in their seats. There were still another two hours left in their trip, as confirmed by his pocket watch.

The whisper returned, and he could make out two words.

Stop here.

His ears worked hard in his old age, and he strained to listen once more. The train was beginning to slow and he could see the desertscape through his window coming clearer into view. It was noon, and the heat sent off waves, forming mirages that only confused him more. The terrain far beyond blurred in waves that looked almost like water in the distance.

Stop. Here.

Why on earth would he stop here? In the middle of nowhere with hardly anything to offer a man like himself?

Albert couldn't imagine there would be much in the way of amenities in Quemar of all places, besides maybe someone to bed in a whorehouse. An establishment he wouldn't dare be caught in, but would most certainly pay one of his men to procure a lady from. No, he thought, it would be a waste of time. He had more important matters to attend to.

Oil.

Oil?

He looked out once more. The ground was cracked and begging for water, the only vegetation some scattered cacti that looked more like shriveled, gray clay.

Could there be oil here?

Albert kicked Mariano's boots.

"Do we know anyone with rigs up here? In Quemar?"

Mariano and Robert woke, their eyes sunken and heavy from their slumber.

"Um, no, no, I don't believe so," Mariano replied quickly, stretching his arms above him.

"This here's a wasteland," Robert interjected, clearing his throat. "No one's out here but maybe some ranch hands. There's no profit with no people."

Oil.

Davenport.

Like hell was he going to lose another site to Davenport, the bastard. In the past two years, the man had gotten his filthy claws into every land of interest to Albert, filing the paperwork before

Albert could even think to speak to his lawyers. Davenport was always one step ahead of him.

Albert considered the voice in his head. If he was right about this, he would follow this voice into the pits of hell as long as he came out with more cash than when he went in.

He collected his items just as the car attendant announced they were stopping.

"Gather your belongings, gentlemen." Albert nearly tripped as he ran off the train, his tie making it near hard to breathe properly as he did so, though he couldn't remember having retied the knot. "I have a good feeling about this place."

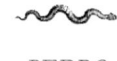

PEDRO

Eighty cents.

That was how much Pedro was worth to his father at only thirteen years old.

Eighty cents and no guarantee that he would return from accompanying these strangers into the desolate desert lands beyond their town. There was no discussion, no chance for Pedro to plead his case and remind his father that all that lay outside of Quemar was a wretched place.

No man who wandered out there didn't come back a little deranged—talking of spirits or animals hung sacrificially on the rock faces, or even reporting bodies of people who were never found upon return.

But his father saw only the silver coins, his eyes widening with a familiar look, the same as when that bitter drink was placed in front of him. Surely he would run off to the tiny saloon down the beaten path and spend the rest of his day and sanity there. By nightfall, Pedro had no doubt every single coin would be in someone else's pockets.

"Pa," Pedro whispered, eyes wide, "es el lugar del diablo."

His father stared harshly down at his son, his bloodshot, tired eyes narrowing. Without a word, he smacked Pedro over the head and pointed him toward the stables. There was no fighting back.

Pedro tried not to think about it as he saddled his horse, tightening the straps and brushing a shaky hand along Tierra's chestnut coat. He couldn't look her in the eyes. Never once had he taken her past the outskirts of town, and never, ever west.

His lips trembled as he lifted himself onto the saddle, feeling the familiar leather reins in his calloused hands. He wondered how many doors these rich men had knocked on before his father answered and accepted their offer.

How many of his neighbors hid behind chairs and tables, hoping the men would leave and find another home to disturb? How many looked upon these visitors, with their wild eyes and black hearts, and refused to lead them through the barren desert?

His heart thundered in his chest and sweat dripped down from his temples, the knots in his stomach tugging fiercely as the seconds passed.

The purple, pink hues of the dawn crested the edge of nowhere beyond the hills and tumbleweeds in the distance. It was the same sky that greeted him every morning of his life, and somehow today it seemed to bid him farewell. He gave Tierra a gentle nudge with his boot, and she silently began to move toward the men.

He thought of all the tales told to him as a child, of men who sought refuge in Quemar and conjured up blasphemous gods to seek revenge on their enemies. Or those of witches who lured men into the desert to wander blindly for all eternity, burning their feet to seared flesh on the scorched, unforgiving land. The town's children reported sightings of a dark angel who would linger at their bedroom windows, scratching the glass with long, sharp nails, beckoning them out with a gentle, melodious tone.

As a boy, the stories kept Pedro awake long into the night, fearful of the places his dreams would take him to, a mind running amuck with vivid images of shadows and bodies being consumed by the damned.

Pedro's throat was dry and he tried to swallow as he wiped the sweat from his brow. He looked out to the desert again. It was hot already and the sun had barely risen from its nightly slumber. Its golden rays stretched weakly in the distance, illuminating the mirages that lingered beyond. It seemed to beckon him as the shadows of the desert willows cast long, dark nets on the ground. He hoped that he would return before nightfall.

*

Pedro rode his horse through the village, wary of these rich men who needed his guidance and his father's horses. If Pedro wasn't certain his father would beat him senseless for turning down the money, he would have rejected their offer at once. Folklore or not, he was not ready to chance death that day.

The three men who followed close behind him told him they were searching for black gold.

"Deep in the desert. We know it's hiding here," one of them said. He had red hair and a knot in his tie that seemed to strangle his neck. It was a wonder he could speak.

Pedro only nodded and didn't ask any questions. Questions risked prolonging their journey.

A few of the town's children peeked out from their tiny makeshift homes, staring at them as they rode by. So early in the morning, and still they had certainly been up for hours working in the unforgiving heat. Their little faces, dirty and tired as if they had labored enough for seven lifetimes, followed the riders like ghosts in the windows until they were out of sight.

Quemar was rather small and home to a few dozen families, plus the strays who had ventured in over the years, too tired to continue trekking through the desert, or without the money and wherewithal to stow away on a train and leave this godforsaken place.

The train station, constructed decades ago, was placed in the hopes that tiny villages like Quemar would attract new settlers and bolster the economies and agricultural industries out west. But as the years passed, Quemar would remain a neglected spot on the map, only identifiable by the lonely train station that stood among the cacti in the middle of the desert. Even the town itself was miles away and tucked beyond the horizon, long forgotten.

The townspeople operated out of the necessity of survival. Beneath the cloudless, rain-starved skies, their bodies burned to the land until their feet became dusty roots in the desert soil. And over time, thoughts of life beyond this land were nothing more than short-lived fantasies to distract them from the never-ending labor.

Mothers tended to the children, their monotonous days and sleepless nights sending them into madness and fever dreams of freedom. Fathers would neglect their duties to visit the town's lone saloon, wasting away their potential and quenching their anger with drinks that stewed in the summers and festered in the hot winters. To children like Pedro, it seemed the land favored the drink of men and had rid itself of cool water long ago. The barkeep's pours never ran dry, but the town well certainly did.

Bodies were not meant to last in such heat.

And yet, somehow, they did in Quemar.

No one they passed in town spoke to the group, but they surely stared. Their eyes narrowed at the men in their fancy, unbroken boots, led by Gustavo's son, who looked like he'd pissed himself twice over. Whatever these people were up to, they wanted no part of it. Especially as they noticed they moved west, into *those* lands.

May god have mercy on them.

The group approached the last house on the outskirts of the town, which was gray and tattered, in desperate need of repairs. Pedro tried to ignore *La Vieja*, the old, feeble woman who owned the home, as she rested in a rocking chair and eyed them warily.

Her skin was ashy and severely wrinkled, the crevices of her face deeply carved like the rough, ridged grooves of tree bark. She narrowed her misty, glassy eyes at them, pursing her lips into a thin line.

"No la mires," Pedro instructed the men as they passed her, one by one along the neglected, dirt road.

Pedro knew of La Vieja by the rumors that had manifested over the years. No one knew the truth of how she came to be or where she'd come from, but one thing was agreed upon in the lore: years of solitude had driven La Vieja mad, and she only left her home at night to terrorize the townspeople who disturbed her in the day. At least, that's what most believed.

She never hosted visitors, and was only ever seen on her front porch, sending people away with her crazed antics. Many believed her to be a spirit, watching over the people of Quemar and punishing those who dared stray out of place. Pedro once heard his abuela claim that she was the reason no one could leave.

Pedro wasn't sure, but he never dared to try and find out.

At least, not until today.

La Vieja's hands rested on the arms of her chair, which seemed to be barely held together with twine. She wore a faded long-sleeved blue dress with a high collar and a frayed, ripped hem that barely touched her bare, callused feet. Her braided hair fell down the front of her body past her chest in long, peppered strands that looked more like straw. It was as if she had sat there for centuries, unmoving except for the minute details of her face and her head as she craned her neck to get a good, long look at the riders moving before her. The windows behind her were broken in shards, and a portion of her roof, caved in and splintered, could be seen through the pane. Each board of wood that had been affixed together to form the walls of the house was rotted and gnarled, giving the entire home a chilling, abandoned look.

A small gust of wind caused the old woman's chair to rock slightly back and forth. It squeaked in protest and the motion revealed different parts of her face, which were illuminated by the morning light that filtered through the battered pergola of her porch. She began to draw her lips upward toward her cheeks, revealing a dark gaping hole between red gums where her teeth should have been. Her dried, cracked lips began to bleed with the smile and she started to laugh, deranged and deep, as if another voice had replaced what should have been hers.

The scene unsettled the men, who avoided her gaze and rushed to distance themselves from the maddening sound of her sinister howling. As the last of them passed, she leapt off the chair with a burst of sudden energy, stopping short of her porch steps in a fit of hysterics as she hooted and pointed at the strangers hurrying away.

Minutes later, only the sound of her laughter echoed distantly in the stillness of the air. Pedro looked up from Tierra, patting her comfortingly, as he took in the vast land ahead. The place that belonged to Quemar on a map he saw once, but was nowhere near welcome—or perhaps, the people were not welcome there. He did not believe in a god, but nor did he want to risk angering one if it did indeed exist. Under his breath, he muttered the all too familiar prayer he would hear on Sundays drifting from the town's small church.

"...*Santa María, Madre de Dios, ruega por nosotros, pecadores, ahora y en la hora de nuestra muerte. Amén.*"

*

The sun, high in the three o'clock sky, scorched the earth unrelentingly, casting long shadows across the dead vegetation that was sparsely scattered around them and the lifeless cacti that stretched short of the heavens. The air was still under the blue, cloudless sky and not a single gust of wind passed through them, leaving the tumbleweeds stranded in place. Far off, cracked earth gave way to mirages and hills that looked as if they could be mountains even further away.

After venturing for miles, they passed an abandoned shack made of corroded wood and a missing roof. It had most likely housed the various madmen who braved the desert solitude, but it was evident they'd never made it out alive, what with the scattered bones and a skull that looked as if something had stepped on it, crushing off a large piece.

Pedro felt sick.

The flat ground stretched for miles, and the only other sign of life was a single vulture spiraling above them. It would circle their group and disappear into the distance before returning to see if any of them had dropped dead of heat exhaustion. It was disappointed each time.

It took them longer than expected to make it out this far—the horses were acting out of character, bucking their riders and trying to turn back to the town for most of the short journey, despite the men rallying to calm them down. Albert remained steadfast that the oil was still a distance away, and Pedro began to worry that their journey risked seeping into the night.

Quemar called out to him. He could feel it in his bones, that unsettling, haunting feeling he got whenever he took Tierra out for a ride and would see the barbed wire fences bordering the edge of the town. It didn't want him to leave. It never wanted him to leave. And he wondered if that feeling was mutual among the other townsfolk or if it was him alone it called to when his thoughts strayed to towns much bigger than his and people much kinder than his father. He wondered if it wanted him safe, or if it wanted him to know it could see him wherever he went. Even if that meant into this land, where things died and the sun burned their flesh alive for the vultures to pick at.

The men turned to Albert often, expectantly waiting for the signal to rally around him, or better yet, to turn around. Mercifully, it was after two and a half hours of riding that Albert finally ordered the group to stop.

Pedro heard and felt the collective sigh of relief as each of them watched their leader clamor off his steed. The sudden halt unnerved the horses, who began to neigh and buck wildly again, now keeping most of the men occupied. Pedro watched as Albert walked toward one of the cacti and took out a pocketknife. In a single swipe, he cut off its arm, which fell and obliterated into dust at his feet. He tapped the dirt with his shoe in different areas and Pedro's mind wandered off.

He looked out and saw only mirages and illusions in each direction. It was isolated—they were isolated—out here beneath the too blue, too barren sky. Pedro wondered how long someone had ever managed to live out here on their own. This thought led his mind to dark musings about all the graves they could be walking over, standing over, at this very moment. Sweat dripped down the sides of his temples and he wiped it with the back of his hand.

Bodies, bodies, everywhere.

Shouts and cheers of amazement pulled him back from his reverie, and he witnessed the men huddled around Albert. They kept pointing at his boot in fascination, talking about the black gold and celebrating with raucous whoops.

Pedro couldn't understand why. He saw nothing but dirt, dirt, and more dirt. No liquid, no gold, nothing that would indicate anything about the land that they hadn't already seen.

He watched the men with a stunned curiosity.

Mariano went to his hands and knees, grabbing fistfuls of dirt and letting it sift through his fingers. The other, Robert, began kissing the ground like a newborn baby. Albert, the one with red hair and the choking tie, retrieved a handkerchief from his back pocket and wiped his hands, grinning wide.

"This is fertile Texas tea, gentlemen, and it's ready for Canterbury & Associates to take hold!" he declared, raising his handkerchief high in the air.

The men responded with more celebration.

And Albert began to dance.

It almost appeared as if they were summoning something, like the stories he'd heard the town children whisper when he was younger. A bizarre jig on a desert grave, beckoning something unholy and wicked.

A horrible uneasiness rose within Pedro.

Neither this land nor these rich men's business deals interested him, and under this godforsaken heat and the eerie feeling of being watched, he wished that they would just hurry the hell up so they could get back to town.

Outside of the group's celebrations, it was too still out here. And with the exception of the ghoulish vultures, no signs of the usual desert creatures had appeared. No bird calls, no insects, not even a scared snake slithered across their path. It was nothing but dead earth. As if God himself desecrated this land and left it to die in seclusion and neglect.

And these rich men relished it.

Pedro only wanted to take off to Quemar before sundown, when he was sure the wickedness of this place would take hold, potentially trapping them here to die like in the stories or the shack they'd passed. Or worse.

He didn't want to think about what *worse* meant.

More sweat dripped from his temples and Pedro wiped it with his raggedy sleeve. As he did, the sweat blurred his vision momentarily, and he could have sworn that he saw Albert and a figure—tall and shadowlike with an enormous black hat covering the upper half of its face—dancing in circles around each other. Fire began to spread across the figure's body and flesh began to melt from its bones, smiling as it danced with Albert.

They were summoning something!

Dread gripped Pedro's insides, and he wiped his eyes to check again for good measure. But this time it was only Albert, dancing in a circle by himself.

"El diablo," he muttered quietly.

He didn't trust waiting around this place anymore, and he made to urge the men to hurry back as the afternoon began to come to a close. As he looked at the crew, he noticed the horses had begun to froth at their mouths, even Tierra panting heavily under him. He jumped off, giving her a break from his weight, and with her reins in hand, turned toward the men with the intent of returning home.

As he took his first step, a sudden sense of vertigo washed over him, and he could hear nothing but the beating of his heart, loud and thunderous in his ears. He fell to the ground in a dizzying disarray and his eyes now beheld a much different scene in front of him.

The desert was absent of the rich men and the horses. Instead, the dead bodies of hundreds littered the desecrated land, all piled on top of each other in fleshy heaps. The putrid smell of death and iron overwhelmed his nostrils as he observed the varying states of decay.

He was frozen with horror on the burning ground as he took in the spectacle before him, the details becoming clearer with each passing second. Humans and animals intermingled in a depraved fashion. It was unnatural, unholy, how the people were ripped apart and thrown asunder both on top and underneath the carcasses of desert beasts.

Try as he might, Pedro could not rip his gaze from what lay before him. He took in every painstaking detail as fear gripped him and clenched his insides.

The bodies, the bodies were everywhere.

He began to writhe and shake from the terror that consumed him, unable to control his movements from the blistering ground.

Oh, the ground was hot indeed, and he could hear the searing of his skin melding with the cracked earth that began to break apart under him, freeing crackles of fire from the depths of the undergrowth. It spit at him relentlessly, burning him, charring his exposed body.

This was not a place of this world, but a hell in the desert that began to expose itself.

Pedro cried out in pain, trying again and again to force his body up, to escape the ground that held him as if it never intended to part. Through the tears of his anguish, a mirage came into view and within it, the dancing figure from earlier made its way toward him. It was small at first, only a speck in the distance that grew steadily larger as it closed the space between them, its body gangly and unrhythmic in the absence of music. The dead bodies began to awaken, crawling or walking clumsily with missing limbs and disproportionate anatomies to create a path for their demented leader.

It came closer and closer until the only thing Pedro could do was pray aloud, any and every prayer that was known to him. He could not run, and he could not move away—he was becoming one with the ground, another body that this land had taken prisoner. Something for the vultures to peck and pull at with their weathered, sharp beaks, satisfying their hungry bellies with his flesh. He could hear their guttural, hissing calls to their brethren as they drew near, fighting voraciously to see which would reach him first.

"¡Ayúdame!" he begged as his voice finally found purchase through the pain.

The dancing creature finally reached him, its face no longer obscured by the large hat it wore. It was La Vieja.

Her body's movements were far different to the ancient face before him, her limbs erratic, demonic, even, twisting like vines. Pedro knew, deep within his soul he knew, that this being before him was the work of something far beyond this earth.

It was worse than the legends any of the town children could produce from their meager, limited imaginations. Worse than the rumors that flowed through Quemar like the drinks in the saloon. Worse than anything he had ever conjured in his nightmares.

"Quemar."

"Quemar."

Pedro would have gladly traded places with the men cursed by witches or those damned by the native gods. Anything besides lying here pathetically, begging for a quick death over the excruciating heat and fire that singed him, the torturous pain of the vultures that fed on his body, and the evil, shrill laugh of La Vieja as she watched.

ALBERT

The oil—how it dripped from his hands. So rich it was. And how much richer he would be when he drilled it. Albert could barely contain his pleasure, dancing and celebrating with Mariano and Robert at his side.

He did not notice how dusk was settling, nor how hot his feet felt as he stepped in some made up rhythm on the ground.

He did not notice the vultures circling once more in larger volts than before.

And he certainly did not notice how their borrowed horses had abandoned them, escaping toward the village.

No, all he knew in that moment was that he would be very rich indeed.

And that Davenport Industries would regret ever stepping in his way.

After a few moments of celebration, Robert rushed past him, screaming.

Albert turned to the man, and he could not believe his eyes.

Robert ran aimlessly into the desert, his entire body shrouded in flames and smoke. He screamed for help, but it was far too late. Robert made it scarcely more than a hundred feet before his body collapsed and the vultures, desperate for flesh, surrounded him and smothered the flame with their wings as they tried to taste a morsel of a man on fire.

The whole spectacle lasted mere minutes and soon Robert was another pile of bones in the desert, picked clean by these ungodly creatures.

"¡Ayúdame!" a voice yelled, and Albert, stunned in fear and

silence, did not answer it.

Mariano instead took off toward the boy from whence the pleas came. His horse was the only one remaining, and the boy was on the ground, trembling.

"What the hell?!" Albert finally managed, racing to them. The boy was in Mariano's arms and looked to be in bad shape, spooked and blistered from lying on the scalding, cracked earth.

"He's hurt!" Mariano yelled.

"How did Robert—how did the boy—" Albert had never been so terrified in his life. Not when he was robbed on the train to Texas as a young man, not when he was caught cheating in blackjack years later, desperate and strapped for cash in Dallas, and especially not when he was held at gunpoint by a disgruntled worker back in Houston. None of those moments held a candle to the evil he was witnessing before him.

"I don't know, he just—he just burst into flames. Out of nowhere," Mariano stammered, his lips trembling as he turned to see the wake of vultures still picking at the bones, looking for any piece of meat left behind after their unnatural feast.

"We need to leave, now," Mariano urged, lifting the boy to his feet. "Let's get what's left of Robert's body on the horse and go! We can make it before nightfall."

Albert's eyes shifted to where Robert's body lay, and he was not ashamed to admit that Robert was the last thing on his mind. He was a fair man, but not a kind one. And Robert, well, it was too late for Robert now. He flicked his eyes up to the horse that shook and neighed in protest as if waiting for the boy to come back to her. The reins were just behind Mariano.

This horse would not be able to carry all three of them plus a brutalized corpse back to Quemar in time. But it could take one...

"Yes," Albert said slowly, "you get the body and I will help the boy onto the horse."

Mariano stood as if accepting these terms and even started to turn on his heel. Albert was nearly itching to grab the reins. But then Mariano stopped and looked back to Albert as the boy stood next to the horse, heaving weakly.

His eyes followed Albert's hand, which he'd instinctively raised toward the reins when he thought Mariano was turning.

"You mean to leave us here, don't you?"

Albert swallowed but did not move his hand from where it lingered halfway between the reins and himself. "Of course not. We're partners."

It happened too quickly. Mariano reached for the inside of his waistband and Albert pushed him, gripping the reins and throwing his body on top of the horse. The boy was shoved aside in the scuffle, shouting as he fell back to the ground.

Albert had the reins and even kicked the horse hard, but then a gunshot rang in his ears and echoed through the desert.

The horse fell, and Albert fell with it.

PEDRO

Pedro couldn't believe his eyes.

Mariano shot Tierra dead in front of him. It was clear the man was aiming for Albert and missed just barely, as Albert's cheek bled where the bullet grazed him. A mere inch and Albert would have been the one dead on the desert floor instead.

With whatever strength he could muster, Pedro ran to Tierra, falling on her dying body and crying out for his beloved horse.

Mariano appeared next to him, pulling Pedro behind him and aiming the gun at Albert, who straightened to stand only a few feet away.

"So, it's come to this, *partner*."

"Whoa." Albert raised his hands. "I didn't mean it. I was scared is all. I would have come back for you two."

Mariano pulled back the gun's hammer. It clicked into place, and all he had to do was pull the trigger. "Bullshit, Albert. You only care about yourself."

Albert let out a nervous laugh and took a step toward them.

"You're right—I have only ever cared about myself. I'm sorry. I-I'm a coward."

Mariano seemed conflicted and Pedro could do nothing but watch as the tension thickened and dusk began to settle. The sun glinted, barely over the horizon in the east, lighting Albert's face in some mixture of fear and excitement.

"And now you will die as a fucking coward."

Albert took another step and Mariano trained the gun square on his head, stopping Albert short. He was within arm's reach now, and Pedro couldn't breathe.

Albert's eyes hardened, but his hands remained raised. "Then before you kill me, tell me this. Was it you who gave the Corpus account to Davenport?"

This question, for some reason, stunned Mariano so badly that he did not move in time to avoid Albert's strike.

The second gunshot rang out.

*

Pedro ran faster than he had ever run before.

He ran past Tierra, who was now being feasted upon by the vultures.

46

He ran past Robert, whose body was already a withering carcass.

And he ran as Albert shouted for him to return. The sound of two more bullets rang out and he felt one whip past his right ear.

Quemar was calling for him, and he intended to answer that call alive.

He was not sure how long he ran for—the journey out into the desert had taken hours by horse, so his sprint back would have barely covered a portion of the distance between him and the town. Every so often, he would turn to look toward where he'd come from and see that Albert faded further into the distance. But soon, darkness fell and with it the shadow that was Albert was eclipsed by the night.

Pedro knew that he was not safe so long as Albert remained out there. And so long as La Vieja, with her promises to take him, lingered alongside the bodies of the land haunting his very thoughts. But his body could barely move anymore, exhaustion and lack of water keeping him from running though he so desperately wanted to.

He looked ahead and saw that he'd made it to the shack they passed early in their journey. Fear of Albert approaching gave him enough bravery to peek inside. It was empty and in much worse condition than La Vieja's home in the village. It appeared as if someone had simply laid piles of wood and broken branches together until it resembled something of a house with a single room and no windows. The roof was mostly missing and the floor was simply the desert, filled with dry dirt and dead cacti.

Pedro made his way inside, listening to the silence. He hated silence, but right now, silence was all he wanted. Silence meant Albert was still far away and that La Vieja would have nothing to dance to.

He was terrified. Even as he lay on the ground and stared up at the starry night sky, he could think only of what awaited him should he leave the safety of the shack in the night. He rested for a short while, just long enough to build his strength.

ALBERT

The desert beckoned him.
It led Albert where he needed to go.
The shack loomed a short distance away.
And he felt reinvigorated.
The dancing woman had visited him.
And promised him all the black gold for his soul.
So he gladly gave it to her.
Just to see that boy suffer.
Because he was fair, but not kind.

PEDRO

Somehow, in all the chaos of the day, Pedro had fallen asleep. He did not even realize it until he heard the sound of footsteps outside the shack. He nearly let out a yelp, but clamped his hand over his mouth and bit down hard on his palm to silence himself. His hands shook uncontrollably, his legs wobbling beneath him.

He was sure he'd peed himself, remembering again the dead bodies and their unholy alliance with the desert beasts. La Vieja and her dance. Albert and his pistol. There were scratching noises around the shed, from Pedro's right, then his left, and then behind him. He whirled, trying to discern where he should expect an impact, but it was all around. No human could be everywhere all at once. Not like this.

He searched the dark ground for anything to defend himself with and found only a piece of dried wood the size of his forearm. It was weak and surely would do nothing to harm Albert if it was him outside the shack. But it was something, and that was the hope Pedro clung to.

"Come out, Pedro. We won't hurt you."

It was Albert.

But who was the *we*?

Pedro remained silent.

There was a loud bang, like a fist knocking against the shack wall.

"Did no one teach you manners, boy?" he hissed. A thousand voices seemed to emanate from Albert as he spoke now.

Pedro held the stick before him, listening as the scratching and knocking began to shift toward the makeshift door of the shack. He could barely think, could barely move, his only thoughts those of Albert and the pistol and La Vieja and the bodies.

"How about you come on out here, and I'll put the gun down. You have my word. Last chance, *amigo*." Albert snickered at the last word, and Pedro dared not move.

"Your funeral, then," Albert said, and without warning, he fired a bullet into the shack. Pedro threw himself to the floor as Albert kicked down the door. The bullet missed its mark, but buried itself inside Pedro's right arm. He cried out, the pain too intense to bear.

Albert entered, watching Pedro with dark, dark eyes.

He lifted the pistol to Pedro and pulled the trigger. Pedro flinched, writhing in pain, but there was only a click.

Albert laughed.

"This here's only got six rounds," he said, lifting the pistol. "Now I know you don't get a lot of schooling here, but let's do some math, hmm?"

He walked closer and Pedro could do nothing but shuffle backwards.

"One for your pretty horse, one for Mariano, two that almost hit you, and one for me," he gestured to a gash in his head, revealing a fragment of his skull. Pedro nearly vomited. "You see, the pretty lady wanted something in exchange for all this fine black gold. It
was an easy tradeoff." He lifted his lips into a grin.

"That leaves us with one. But it seems I just wasted that." Albert gestured to Pedro's right arm. Blood oozed from his wound, the bullet lodged deep in his arm. Agony and pain battled with the fear and adrenaline coursing through him.

Albert tossed the gun aside.

It was quiet again as Albert stared down at Pedro.

"You'll like it here with us," he said as blood trickled down his chin. "We've been waiting for you."

A slow chanting began outside the shack as Pedro stared at Albert's dark eyes and bleeding head.

Quemar.

Quemar.

Quemar.

Albert took a step toward him and Pedro made to scramble back, but his injured arm gave out beneath him. He searched for the flimsy piece of wood, anything he could use to defend himself with his good hand.

Quemar.

Quemar.

Quemar.

La Vieja's cackles echoed outside, getting closer and closer still. Albert stepped again and Pedro grabbed hold of the wood piece and tried to strike him. But it did nothing, as expected. It snapped in two against Albert's leg, not even giving Pedro a moment to run.

Quemar.

Quemar.

Quemar.

Albert bent over Pedro and whispered. His breath was stale and reeked of rot and decay.

"It burns."

Pedro tried to fight him off with his legs and his one good hand, but Albert was too strong. He gripped his neck and began to squeeze. La Vieja was dancing in Pedro's vision now, through the threshold of the shack and into the dark space inside.

Air and sanity were slipping from him, further and further they went.

He saw memories of riding Tierra through the outskirts of town.

He saw how he played with the town children in rare moments of happiness.

He saw himself meeting the rich men for the first time and how peculiar Albert looked to him. With his fiery red hair and his tie that squeezed the space between his head and shoulders.

His tie.

With whatever strength remained, Pedro focused on the tie still wound around Albert's neck. He kneed Albert in the stomach and jumped behind him before he could fight back. Drawing on every bit of anger and fear and frustration, he pulled on that tie so hard he was sure it would snap in two.

But it didn't.

Albert screeched angrily, making the most inhuman, unnatural sounds before he went quiet. Finally, his body went limp in Pedro's arms. Pedro breathed raggedly, terror striking him as he stared at the man he killed lying on the floor. He grabbed the weapon—even without a bullet it was better than a wretched piece of weak wood. He lifted it over his head, ready to use it to strike Albert should he awaken, but dead he remained.

The dawn was approaching. Pedro could see it through the open roof as purple, pink, and black hues fought for a piece of the sky. He turned to leave, and his blood ran cold.

In all the madness of the moment, he had forgotten about La Vieja, who now stood blocking the only way out of the shack.

She stared at him from beneath her large black hat, her wrinkled face apathetic as she beheld him.

He trembled before her.

And she continued to stare.

He dropped the pistol and let it hit the ground with a thud.

She took a step to the side, no longer blocking the doorway.

He swallowed, feeling the blood from his wound weeping down his fingertips, dripping onto the earth.

But still, she stared.

He took a step.

Then another.

And another.

OBLIVIOUS

"So, you said you were from Portland, right?"

The voice was warped and garbled, almost dreamlike to the disoriented Daniel, who tried to shake his head no. He stumbled slightly from the dizzying motion of walking, or at least he believed he was walking. He had to be, or else there wouldn't be anything for his legs to stumble on. He could hear the sound of gravel beneath his sneakers and the crrruncccchh it made as he lost his footing. He could make out a running trail in the darkness, long and curved, nestled within trees. Nothing more.

"Whoa there," the voice called to him. It sounded far away, as if it were calling out to him from the tiptop of a football stadium, like the one erected at his old high school back home. There, the stadium steps were steep, and at least a couple of times a year, there would be an incident where a student or family member slightly injured themselves, mainly from embarrassment, as they fell down those steps.

Just like he was doing now, falling down, down, down. Except there weren't any steps, at least none that he could feel. It was only him and the ground, set to come together in an outstanding force of motion that would only bring pain.

Distantly, he was aware that he should brace himself, lift his arms defensively to absorb the impact, but his thoughts and actions were lazy and disconnected. A slight chuckle escaped his lips as he imagined himself falling onto a cloud like they did in the cartoons, how fluffy and pillowy, and he began to welcome the idea of meeting the earth beneath him. No sooner had he laughed than two heavy, strong hands were on him, breaking his fall and holding him upright. The person placed one of his hands over their shoulder, steadying him and taking the bulk of his weight.

"Hey, you don't look so good," the voice said, and Daniel laughed harder. The way the voice elongated its words was comical, almost cartoon-like.

When did things become so funny?

How did he get here?

Living in a decently sized college town in an otherwise desolate part of the state left a lot of room for people to wander. And that's all Daniel wanted to do—wander outside of the crowded Portland city and see what small town living offered.

"You're funny," Daniel remarked.

"That's because we're friends now, aren't we buddy?" The voice was becoming clearer now. "We're almost there, just under this bridge."

The words were beginning to register in the foggy brain of Daniel Lanzo. The bridge appeared as bits and pieces of his vision that meshed together like watercolors in a Picasso painting behind a cloud of gray mist.

What could he even remember?

Natalie Muli's twenty-first birthday party.

The invitation was on thick, black cardstock, decorated in gold glitter. In truth, Daniel was surprised to receive one at all.

Natalie, with her dazzling smile and dark hair with highlights that ran through it like streaks of sunshine. He was surprised she even knew he existed outside their two classes.

And even more surprised that she wanted him to see her.

He skipped studying for once and allowed himself to enjoy the nightlife he'd so casually ignored most weekends over the course of four years. It was the last semester of his senior year. He resolved to end on a fun note, and this party was the perfect excuse. No more late nights in the company of Folgers and Hot Pockets, no siree.

The voice was now agitating Daniel with its continuous loop of questions that felt unnecessary to respond to.

Are you from Portland?

I always wanted to visit Portland.

Portland.

Portland.

Portland.

It droned on and on.

"If I didn't live in Portland," Daniel hiccupped, "why would I be here?" It made no sense, but in his head it did, and that's all that mattered.

"Okay," the voice replied, "just keeping conversation."

It grunted under Daniel's body, which felt like dead weight he could no longer fully control. His legs were slipping out from under him again, and if the voice didn't have a firm grasp on his upper body, Daniel surely would have met the dirt.

They continued forward to a destination Daniel could not process in the fog that muddled his thoughts, and soon he felt the ground shift to a wobbly, solid surface. He tripped and fell sideways into a tree. The bark scratched his face, and while he knew it must have hurt, he felt nothing but a tingling sensation on his cheek. The voice pulled him onto a damp plastic object. He just wanted to go to sleep—everything was too fuzzy.

It rocked gently and Daniel was floating into space. The rocking sensation mirrored the back and forth of his memory, flipping between the blurred images that slowly came back to him.

Taking free shots at the bar.

Dancing with Natalie.

Taking more shots.

Daniel holding Natalie's phone to take a video of her birthday countdown and the cake that was presented to her. The numbers 2 and 1 were each connected to a long, golden sparkler candle that jutted from the center of the round, white cake. The sparklers danced along with the tiny flame that flickered at the top, showering the cake like a golden firework. She blew out her candles and smiled straight into the camera, through the camera, at him.

She's looking at *me*, he thought.

She blew a kiss into his camera and the others that faced her. He liked the feeling of her smiling at him, blowing kisses at him. He wondered how it would be to kiss her.

"Do you think Natalie likes me?" he asked aloud.

"Sure, sure," the voice answered. "We're almost there now. Hurry or Natalie won't come see you."

Daniel smiled dreamily.

Natalie was beautiful, wearing a short-sleeved black dress with a sash over her that read: *I'm 21! The Wait is Finally Over!*

Her hair was parted down the center and curled this time, and he admired that she took the time to try something new. Her silver hoops shimmered under the bar lights, reflecting her perfect smile.

He felt a moist sensation in his socks and wondered briefly if he'd peed himself. He reached an unsteady hand to check his crotch. It was dry.

"Now, Daniel," the voice called out. It was far away again. "Is there anything you want to be remembered by? Anything you want the world to know? I'm giving you five seconds, that's it."

"I didn't think you'd come," Natalie whispered in his ear as they danced to a slow song.

"I'm surprised you invited me," Daniel admitted.

She smiled shyly. "My friends dared me to."

"Oh," Daniel began to loosen his grip on her waist. "I can leave if you want."

"No!" She held on tighter, her hands clasped together behind his neck. "I-I wanted to. I just used them as an excuse."

Her eyes, god, her eyes. He could see now the meaning of "getting lost" in someone's eyes. They shined beneath the dim lights of the bar. He never realized how many shades of brown there were, that they all blended together to make hers.

For once, he decided to be brave. "You are the most beautiful woman I have ever seen."

Natalie smiled and bit her lip softly. "You must tell all the girls that."

"No," he admitted, "just you."

"Natalie," he whispered, feeling sick.
"She would want you to pay attention."

They stared into each other's eyes, now sharing the same air. Their lips faintly touched. His heart was beating faster than he could handle as he trembled gently with anticipation.

And then the voice called out to him.

He didn't recognize it, but it stopped their kiss.

It needed his help.

Where was Natalie?

"5!"

Now that he thought about it, Daniel wasn't sure he ever asked who the voice was. Daniel's shirt was getting wet. Water was sloshing over the edges of the area where he sat. The haze of his mind was subsiding as he sobered up, but not quite fast enough. He felt that he should be scared, but couldn't figure out why that should be.

"4!"

He couldn't remember when he'd left the party, or how he came to meet the voice. He was soaked all over now, realizing that they must be floating on a body of water. But then that would mean...

"3!"

He wished the voice would just tell him what was happening, that he could think of the proper words to ask. He wished his brain would work as it always had in school. His parents and teachers always assured him that he was destined for great things; the more he achieved, the more they praised him. His brain would take him wherever he wanted to go, which to them meant anywhere in the world.

He was a smart boy, their Daniel.

At this moment, as adrenaline took over, he wanted to go home. Back to Portland, back to noisy traffic beneath the third-floor apartment where his mother and older sisters raised him.

"2!"

"I'm scared," Daniel cried out. He began puking on his lap. His buzz was gone now. Nausea prevailed and the combination of it with his growing fear made him useless. He heard the vomit plop into what he was now sure was water. He tried to pull himself up, dripping with sweat that further muddied his vision. As he wiped his eyes with clammy hands, the realization crept in quickly.

Before him was a stranger on a small kayak barely visible underneath the bridge. The stranger, too, was shrouded in the darkness that befell the lake they floated on. For a moment, Daniel believed him to be a shadow, a dark figure with large human limbs but devoid of a heart or the need for air. His mind ran away with everything it could be, because no person would hurt someone innocent like him, right?

But it wasn't a nightmare. It was real. And his cloudy, fogged, useless brain came to terms with three things:

Daniel didn't know how to swim.

He was drunker than he had ever been before.

He was stranded with a stranger on a large lake.

"1!"

There was nothing but silence far in the distance, and he finally admitted how much he hated the quiet out here. He cried out and soiled his underwear like a bedwetting child afraid of thunderstorms that rattle and shake the house. He was young, only twenty-two, and with a whole life before him that he would never come to know.

His mother may never recover—she would blame herself and suffer as only a mother could at the loss of her beloved son. And he could see her buried six feet under alongside his body in one of the many city cemeteries. The laborious strain of welcoming him into the world felt both so long ago, and also not long enough.

He was sick, dizzy and sick, and no one came at his cries.

"And blast off," the stranger whispered with vigorous excitement, and overboard Daniel went, plummeting into the frigid lake that swallowed him greedily.

It happened so quickly that he barely registered the kayak rowing out of sight. He was a human anchor attached to nothing, his drunken body sinking into the never-ending abyss. The light of the night sky dimmed ever so gradually from view until he was truly alone within the lake's belly of darkness. He thrashed and clawed, but soon the earthy tendrils that stretched out from the bottom entangled him. His throat burned with a fiery vehemence; he wouldn't make it to the surface in time. Even so, against all odds and all hope, his will to live overpowered the reality of his circumstances, and as his body shut down, his mind went into overdrive.

He dreamed of the people he loved the most. Happy memories of his life flashed before him like the polaroid snapshots in his mother's photo albums.

He knew at that moment he could have loved Natalie, and only wished that he would've taken the chance to kiss her, hold her longer, be with her again.

He imagined a world in which he had such courage. To not let the outside world in, to not listen to the voice in his head.

And in his imagination, she would kiss this city boy for the world to see and not care what they thought. They could have been wrapped in each other's arms, excited at the start of something new together.

At least, that's how he believed it could have gone, before he surrendered to the eternal slumber that was his fate.

His corpse lingered at the bottom of the lake, entangled in the trash and cyanobacteria that occupied it. Swaying softly with the slow movement of the current as if he were a baby being soothed to sleep by mother nature.

Alone

in

a

world

that

was

oblivious

to

his

death.

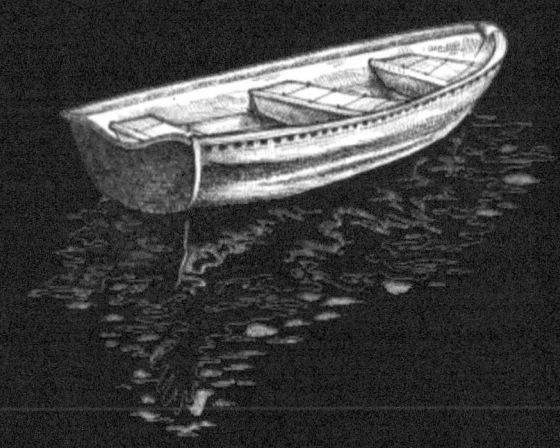

THE HIKE

THE BLOOD TRICKLES DOWN THE RIVERBED. IT POISONS the water and smells of iron and decay. It flows slowly into the creek. The crystal blue water mixes with the red of wounds that do not heal. The earth groans painfully, the dirt trembles, the trees shake in fear.

Oh, how it aches.

Oh, how it longs to satisfy its hunger.

Can you feel it?

Beneath your palms, press it there in the soil—listen as it begs for more. Its cries a shrill echo in the wind, carried into our homes and through our dreams as we sleep, until we can feel it too. We wake from our slumbers with pain so intense we wander into the wilderness barefoot and naked to beg for mercy.

Oh, how we have failed.

Oh, how we have failed.

It claws at the roots and drags us under.

Our offerings are worthless and cast asunder.

It is rising to punish us all.

We must make things right.

Or soon.

So very soon, you shall see what happens.

When it wakes in wrath.

"Now, take a right at the creek and stick to the beaten path for about a mile or two. It's the shortcut to Hiker's Village, where you'll meet Marge, the camp attendant. She'll get your info and set you up for the night."

"Thank you," I say, nudging Aaron to do the same.

He mumbles some sort of response to the elderly couple who sit in their camping chairs next to their impressive, albeit dirt-stained, tent. They look as if they've grown roots in this nest of the woods, so comfortable are they as they tend to their mid-afternoon flame, not even bothering to wave at the mosquitos that run rampant around us. Not a single bug spray in sight. The insects seem to be bored of the couple, too.

"Is this your first time hiking us in these parts?" the woman asks, taking a sip from her water bottle.

Aaron gives a noncommittal shrug. "I might have come this way once before."

"What about you two? Do you come here often?" I ask quickly, ignoring Aaron's curt reply.

The couple assesses us warmly, and the woman responds, "We live in the neck of these woods. Every so often we like to come out here and spend some time talking with the hikers."

"Oh, that's neat."

"It sure is," the man replies. "If you're ever up for simple living, this here's the spot to be."

"Maybe one day," I says. The conversation is lasting longer than I'd like it to and while it's still morning, I very much want to get situated at the camp site before the afternoon settles. "Hope to see you around soon. Thanks again!"

The couple smiles and offers parting sentiments.

We continue on our way.

"That was nice of them," I say, fumbling with my backpack straps. Twenty pounds doesn't sound too heavy, but after a half hour on my back, it's starting to weigh on me. "I told you that asking for directions wasn't so hard."

Aaron rolls his eyes. "Yeah, but how do you know they aren't serial killers?"

I turn to give a final wave to the couple, who sit in their folding chairs tending to the little fire. They have to be in their sixties at least. I'm sure they're showing off to young adults like us that they have the expertise to do such things without trouble.

"You're right, he could beat me in a footrace, easily." Aaron clicks the key fob twice, and we hear our car lock from a short distance away. "I'm just saying, you should be more careful."

"Oh, yes, she looked absolutely feral."

"I'm serious."

"And so am I." I buckle the pack's chest strap. "Isn't it best practice to make sure people see us in case a bear attacks us or something?"

"How would that save us from a bear attack?"

"I don't know, give me a minute."

He smiles down at me as we head for the creek. "Thanks for coming. I know how much you hate being outdoors."

"I don't hate it. I just have an understanding with nature. It leaves me alone and I leave it alone."

"So what made you change your mind?"

"It's been a while since we've had a weekend alone. I thought this would be romantic or something." A mosquito buzzes by my ear as I say the words, and I swat at it. "But let's go to the beach next time."

"Deal."

The last time I went camping, I was nine years old. It was at some state park I couldn't recall the name of, but I did remember my father lying next to me and my brother and pointing out the stars. He would show us all the constellations he knew by heart, and I would pretend to see them, when really all I noticed was how it all looked like glitter. I told myself that the moon liked to get dressed in style, adorned with stars that sparkled like jewels, and that the sun was jealous. I'm not sure why, but picturing it made me giggle then and even now as I walk next to Aaron.

I don't remember much else from my first camping trip. We may have hiked, we may have just sat by the water and eaten bologna sandwiches and a bag of potato chips, but the dressed-up night sky? Now that I remember.

But that was then.

Now, years later, me and my on again-off again boyfriend hike next to each other looking for the designated camp site. The GPS is not forest friendly, and after an hour of driving aimlessly through Snohomish County trying to find it, we—or Aaron, rather—settled on parking and hiking our way there instead. He said it would be an
adventure to walk through the wilderness like Frodo and Sam, though I expect it's because he was tired of being cooped up in the car after hours of driving into the Middle-of-Nowhere, Washington.

And to no one's surprise, we were lost in the first thirty minutes.
It took us nearly twice as long to make it back to our car. And over ten minutes of petty arguing to convince him that we needed to ask for directions.

He would never admit he was lost, though.

And I wanted to salvage the rest of this trip.

"So, what made you ask me to come along?" I nudge him playfully.

He turns and nudges me back. "I didn't want to go alone and you were the first name I thought of."

"I'm sure you say that to all the girls."

"Only the ones I like." He brings me in and squeezes my shoulders.

I can hear the creek, the flowing water not too far away. In the northwest, summers have a brief four-to-six-week period where rain only teases instead of being guaranteed and the sweltering heat feels humid and thick. The path we walk is slightly damp and I can hear the occasional squish of my feet in the mud. The paths here are definitely not used often—they look rather neglected, and some of the weeds make their way through the dirt and obscure sections of the trail as we walk farther into the woods.

Sweat trickles down my forehead to my neck in little beads as we push past clusters of brush and low hanging branches. The only silver lining is the evergreens, yawning up to the sky and shading our bodies from the hot sun.

The sounds of the creek grow nearer, but I still can't see it.

"Do you think it's much further?"

"Yeah, I hear it just up ahead."

It sees all.

Eyes entangled with the moss and trees and rock. It crosses the threshold between sky and earth, lingering in the air and tasting of bitterness.

Can you taste it, too?

There on your tongue—can you taste it, I said?

It's moving, summoning us all to do its bidding.

This anger, oh this anger.

Oh, how we have failed.

Can you feel it in the trees?

The way the branches shiver and shake in the wind, the bark peeling down and revealing its naked truths.

Time is of the essence.

We must get ready now.

"It's been over an hour, Aaron. I still don't see it."

I can still hear the creek in the distance, but no matter how long we walk toward the sound, we've yet to stumble upon it or any source of water save for our personal bottles.

"No shit, Briana," he huffs. "Maybe that couple gave you the wrong directions."

"Hey, easy." I turn to him, trying to keep calm. "They seemed confident—"

"And that means they know what they're talking about?"

"No, but—"

"And now we're lost, all because you had to ask for directions." He points at me, his brows raised accusingly.

I've had enough of this, pushing his finger away from me.

"In case you forgot, we were already lost before I even thought to ask for directions. And what's with your shitty attitude?!"

"You just didn't give me a chance!"

"I always give you fucking chances!"

The first time I met Aaron was on the 2 Line riding the rail from Redmond to Bellevue. I had missed the eight a.m. and was forced to wait for the next, running late to work and irritable. When it finally arrived, I got on, plugged my earbuds in and blasted the first thing on my playlist.

He climbed the steps and sat next to me as if he was drawn to my irritability and needed to see me have a laugh or two. He made me laugh and forget about the fact that I was late, and by the end of the ride, he had my number and my hopes that he would call.

Because the Aaron I met that day was all calm and charming, handsome and funny.

He used to be funny.

He didn't used to be this angry.

"Is everything okay here?"

Our heads whip around toward the man speaking. He stands there with his backpack and hiking attire looking very much at ease with himself save for the look of concern as his eyes pass between the two of us.

I glance at Aaron, raising a brow.

He takes a deep breath, not bothering to look at me, though I know for certain he saw my eyes burning into his skull.

"Sorry." Aaron shrugs uncomfortably and scratches at the back of his head as he speaks. "We're just trying to find the camp site. This one older couple told us to walk in this direction and turn at a creek, but we haven't been able to find it. Would you happen to know where it is?"

The hiker pauses for a moment, and then grins. "Ah, not to worry. That happens often out here. I'm headed that way myself. You all must be new at this sort of thing."

"Pretty much," I say.

"It's our first time here is what she means," Aaron says, and I give him a pointed look.

"Of course, this area's known more for boondocking. Everyone kind of makes themselves at home." He bends over to tie his shoelaces.

"It sure seems that way," I say, "but thank you. We really appreciate it, um?"

"Ben," he answers, standing up and pushing back his light brown curls.

"Briana." I shake his hand.

"Aaron." Aaron reaches over and does the same.

"The couple was right—you did have to go toward the creek, but they pointed you in the wrong direction. It's actually more northeast." He points a hand out to our right.

"Ah, yes. That explains it," Aaron says, shifting his backpack.

"Alright, well night can sneak up quick out here, so let's get moving."

It moves slowly, pressing the soil deeper into the earth.
Do you see how the ground trembles as it nears?
It quakes and steadies, quakes and steadies.
Oh, how we have failed.
We will not last long before it.
So, hurry!
There may still be a chance.
If you hurry, we may be granted mercy.

Painless deaths—ah, yes. Painless deaths.

The tension in my body lessens as the sounds of the creek grow louder now with each step. I look up to the sky, barely visible beneath the blanket of trees, and see that it has become clouded and gray. I look at my watch. Half past five o'clock. The last twenty minutes have flown by as Ben chatted away about his morning hike and all the animals he saw along the way—squirrels, a skunk, and an occasional deer.

Now that I think about it, I don't think I saw a single animal on our own trek through the woods.

"So, how often do you hike here?" I ask.

Ben laughs. "Too much. It's a great place to get away from the noisy city."

"Oh neat," Aaron says. "Are you from Seattle?"

"Nah," Ben says. "I live in this area. But I swear the city is so loud it reaches out and grabs you when you just want some peace and quiet."

"I like peace and quiet sometimes." I laugh. "But too much is too much for me. The traffic moving along at night is like white noise to my ears when I sleep."

Aaron takes a sip of his water bottle as we speak, then hands it to me. "Want a drink?"

I take it greedily.

Aaron turns to Ben. "Don't you ever get nervous being out all alone out here?"

Ben shakes his head. "I used to when I was a kid. But I find that the woods and I have become one over the years. You treat the land right and it will treat you right back."

I hand back Aaron's water bottle.

"What about sleeping alone at night? Doesn't it get a little creepy?"

"Oh, I see someone's been reading up on the village lore." Ben laughs.

"I'm a bit of an internet sleuth."

"Really, she is. She can tell you anything about anywhere if you give her five minutes with a book." Aaron smiles. For the first time this entire trip, it seems like things are starting to turn around.

I return his smile, grinning.

"Well, afraid to tell you most of it is hogwash. In all my thirty-six years of living here, I've never once seen anything that made me question reality. As I said before, you take care of the land and it takes care of you right back."

I nod along with Ben, but I glance at Aaron. He stares at me with his soft, brown eyes, so genuine I nearly forget why we were upset to begin with.

I was surprised to see that Aaron called that same afternoon as I walked out of work toward the rail.

Even more surprised to have him ask me to dinner that night and actually bring flowers.

I spent most of the night enjoying his company and the rest of it wondering if someone would run up and point a camera in my face as an obnoxious TV host asked how it felt to be bamboozled.

None of that happened, thankfully, but I still had that feeling as we went on our second and third dates. Those are the first impression dates—the ones where you try to see if there are any cracks in the facade, any notion that the person sitting across from you at a romantic, candlelit dinner is not who they claim to be.

With Aaron, at least the version of him from our early days, it seemed simple enough. I didn't feel like I had to dissect his every move or go on a tirade with my girlfriends trying to figure out if he was really an architect, if he graduated from Washington State University, and if he was dating more than one girl at a time. He was simple and funny and that's all that mattered to me.

I think it happens that way so naturally for most of us. We want so badly for someone to fill the piece of ourselves we think is missing that we convince ourselves that the research is adequate and this person is truly the one. When really, they're meant to be someone who could only temporarily fill the void while we try to remember what got us so off track to begin with.

Because if everything was right between me and Aaron, then I wouldn't be reflecting on all these happy early memories in the midst of struggle and chaos.

Would I?

"Fuck, my watch stopped working." I click the buttons on the side, but the clock face glitches at me.

"And still no service." Aaron looks at his phone. "How much further? It looks like night is going to be here any minute and we still haven't found the creek."

We both stop to stare at Ben, who continues walking forward. I am hyperaware of my surroundings—I can feel the blood pulsing in my veins, the crickets chirping, an owl hooting from nearby, and even the creek so close it feels like we're practically standing in it. Goosebumps rise on my skin.

"Ben?" I ask, trying to sound calm.

He turns to us, looking genuinely confused. "Yes?"

"How much further?" Aaron repeats.

"Not too far now. It's just over this little ridge here and then we take a right for about a mile. Come on."

He turns to move but notices that Aaron and I are both rooted in place.

Something is very wrong about Ben. And something is very wrong about where we are. My stomach clenches.

"Where are you taking us?" Aaron demands, taking a step toward him.

Ben turns to face us, smiling. "To the creek, of course."

"Which creek?" Aaron challenge.

"The one by the camp site." He shrugs. "That's where I'm

headed, at least."

"Look, we don't want trouble. We just want to get there safely, that's all," I say. Tears are forming in my eyes and I can't explain why that is, and maybe that's what makes it worse. I don't know where in this forest we are, and I don't know how to get back to the car even if I wanted to. Night has fallen.

"Good." Ben's grin grows wider. "No trouble here." He takes a step toward me and Aaron immediately cuts in between us.

"Cut the shit. What are you up to?"

"Are you always so abrasive?" Ben tilts his head, inspecting Aaron. "It seems you are angry. These woods don't like angry people."

"What are you—"

Aaron can't finish his sentence before Ben punches him in the face. I scream and fall over a branch as I try to back away. Aaron punches him back; they tussle with each other in the dark. I can barely make out their figures as they shove each other to the ground and against the trees.

I shout uselessly for them to stop.

I rip off my backpack and fervently search for the flashlight I have in there, shoving through clothes and toiletries.

Aaron yells something unintelligible as Ben howls with laughter, and then a gut-wrenching crack sounds in the stillness of the woods.

My breath is shaky, my hands barely able to function as I grip the flashlight.

I don't know if I should turn it on.

I don't know if I need to run.

In the sticky, summer heat of night, I can only feel the sweat dripping over my skin and the goosebumps that refuse to lie back down.

"Briana?"

It's Aaron. Oh my god, it's Aaron.

I flip the flashlight on.

And there on the ground is Ben.

Dead.

Painless death.

You see now?

Painless deaths for those who deserve it.

One for you.

And one for me.

It takes care of us only as well as we take care of it.

It will forgive us for our mortal failures.

The blood is pooling in the water.

The air is thick and heavy.

The offerings are set.

And so it is, too.

"Oh my god, you killed him!" I can't help but scream, my body in utter shock as I repeat those same words again and again.

Ben lies on the dirt, a bloodied rock resting next to him like a makeshift gravestone. I can barely stand, but I'm too afraid to sit next to this body.

Body.

It's a real fucking body.

I drop the flashlight and Aaron rushes to turn it off and shove it in his pocket.

"Shhh, Briana." Aaron covers my mouth and I taste a bit of blood on his fingers. And I puke a little inside my mouth thinking about whether it's his or Ben's. "You need to be quiet, okay." His voice shakes, but he's trying to remain calm. "We don't know where Ben was leading us. What if there's other Bens out there? Do you want them to find us?"

I can't see Aaron's eyes anymore in the dark, but I can feel them pleading with me. And as much as I want to scream and panic, he's right.

What if he was taking us somewhere we wouldn't make it out of?

We've been walking unencumbered for hours. Who knows

where the hell we actually are anymore or what exactly we've stumbled upon.

"Do you understand?" Aaron asks, his hand still over my mouth.

I nod, because that's all I can even do.

"Okay, I'm going to let go, but you have to stick with me, promise?"

I nod again.

He lets me go and I take in a deep breath while my mind screams that there's a body two feet from my foot. I want to vomit, I want to faint, I want to be home under the covers where things like this don't happen to girls like me.

"I didn't mean to kill him," Aaron whisper, a shakiness to his voice. "He attacked me first—he punched me out of nowhere."

"I-I know. I saw." I can't manage anything else.

The body is right there.

"Exactly, exactly." Aaron breathes anxiously, and I grab his hand.

He takes a step toward me and lets out a weak grunt.

"What happened?" I ask, eyes wide and scanning the dark.

"I think I twisted my ankle." He tests it, putting some weight on his left foot, and nearly cries out. "Fuck, that hurts."

"We need to move, now," I say, grabbing what's left of my backpack and shouldering some of his weight.

It takes a few uncoordinated steps until we finally figure out how to walk quickly with his injured ankle.

We're leaving the body behind.

We move quietly for ten minutes before Aaron whispers, "I love you, Briana. I've always loved you."

Aaron has never told me those words before, and I'm too shocked to say them back as we fumble through the wilderness fresh from witnessing my first dead body.

He was never one for sentiments after the fifth date and rarely made time for me after the seventh. Slowly but surely, we drifted apart and I waited by the phone for him to call on weekends hoping that tonight would be the night he missed me.

Sure, we would hook up every now and then, but there were no flowers, no cute dates, and the humor was all but gone. It shriveled up, back to wherever he housed the rest of his disguises for women he was interested in at the moment.

But still, like an idiot. I stayed and convinced myself that it was a mutual decision to play the field and be open to options. Though I didn't keep up my end, if that was even an expectation on his part to begin with.

No, I waited and waited.

Not so patiently rotting on the couch by my phone.

And nearly a month after our last hookup, he finally sent me a text… *Wanna go camping with me this weekend?*

It's nearly pitch black save for the bits of night sky that peek through the trees from above. It's barely enough to light our way and we're both too scared to turn on the flashlight. Fearful of what the light would show us, or that the light would reveal where we are to whoever's out here. That last one almost convinced me to toss it aside and forget it ever existed. But I don't.

I get the horrible sensation that we are being watched and I try—unsuccessfully—to tell myself it's all in my head.

The body.

It's all in my head.

Lying next to me.

It's all in my head.

Eyes. I can feel them taking me in from their hiding spots in the woods. Whatever it is out there is waiting, biding its time for whatever sick pleasure it gets from watching two lost people, desperate and hurt all alone in the woods.

I'm so consumed by my thoughts and the eyes that I know are there that I misstep into a muddy patch of earth and slip, taking Aaron down with me.

"Shit," I say. "Aaron, Aaron are you okay?"

"No," he admits, trying to stand. "It hurts too bad. I can't walk."

Then we hear it. The creek.

No longer is it hidden beyond some arbitrary distance—I can feel the edge of it on my sneakers. I reach my fingers down and feel the rush of the water against them. I bring the water to my face and sip, then wipe my hands and arms with it, unable to control myself. I wipe Aaron with it, too, the sensation cool on our feverish and panicked bodies.

I look at Aaron and whisper excitedly, "We made it to the creek!"

He exhales a sigh of relief. "That means we're only a mile or two away from the camp. If we hurry, we can get there in a half hour."

"Okay, let's get you up."

Hope is fleeting as I try to lift him. His ankle can't bear any weight and I can barely lift him properly anymore, especially not for an entire mile. Panic rises and I feel the air thicken. But most unsettling, I feel the eyes once more.

"Briana." Aaron squeezes my hand. "You're going to have to go to the camp without me."

"What? No, I'm not leaving you here."

I wish that I could admit that I care for him so deeply that I don't want to see him hurt. And that's technically true—I want him safe. I want us both safe. And I also want him with me because I don't want to be alone in these woods with the eyes that pierce into me from between the trees.

Just like I wanted him all those days and nights that I waited, simply because I did not want to be alone. But I ended up alone anyway, didn't I?

Guilt and shame prick at my insides.

"No, I can't move. I need you to run as fast as you can to the camp and get help. Promise me you won't leave me." He holds my hand in a white-knuckled grip. "Promise me."

I nod, barely able to make out his features. "I promise."

I remove my backpack and leave it with him to lighten the load.

And then I take off in a dead sprint.

Ah, it is time!

It is time!

Do you not hear the wind as it howls?

The stars how they shine?

The earth as it grows in strength?

Feel it once more—place your hands here and here.

Do you feel it?

That humming within? It is ready for us.

It forgives us.

Painless deaths.

The time has finally come.

I see a fire in the distance with tents huddled around it in a circle. People are up and mingling about. It must not be as late as I thought it was. I'm crying tears of happiness, streams flowing down my cheeks like the damn creek that took an entire day to find. We're going to make it out of here alive. We're going to go back home and live.

Just fucking live.

I run toward the campers surrounding the fire. I must look like a bat out of hell, screaming for help and startling the children as their parents pull them away from me.

But as I look into the faces of the people around me, my heart drops.

There standing slightly to my left, smiling sweetly, is the old couple from this morning. The woman gives me a small wave, excitement in her kind eyes.

Excitement.

That's the word.

That's what's in the eyes of the people surrounding me.

Because no one is moving to help me.

They're all just smiling at me.

"My boyfriend," I whimper. "He needs help. Th-there's something out there!"

Still no one moves.

"Please!" I beg. "We're lost!"

The older couple begin to bow and the rest follow suit. I glance at each of them, confused and disturbed, until my eyes land on a little girl smiling at me.

No, at something *behind* me.

The feeling of eyes on my skin comes back to me. My breath hitches, my limbs shuddering. I can't help it—I nearly bite my tongue, my teeth and jaw trembling violently.

I know I must turn, at some point I have to turn, because from what I can see, no one here is going to help me. No one here is going to let me leave, are they?

I move my body slowly, turning my head to meet what has been following us in the woods. The eyes creep along my body, sending goosebumps along my flesh, the small hairs on the back of my neck rising. Though nothing can prepare me for what I come face to face with.

My eyes widen and the tears keep flowing. I open my mouth in shock.

Aaron stands there before us all.

Blood covers his entire body as if he's bathed in it. As if it was spread across his torso and on his arms and neck, his face…

It dawns on me as I lift my shaking arms.

They, too, are full of blood.

The creek.

I look back up to Aaron slowly, watching as a smile begins to form. He stands taller now, his weight easily held by both legs. I take a step back.

"I'm not lost," he says, slowly removing my backpack from his shoulders. "You are."

PART II

ARE YOU SLEEPING?

The man faces away from me, tinkering with the cabinets.

I can barely hear him as he mutters words under his breath.

His raspy, anguished tone makes my body go numb,

my breathing heavy.

What is he really saying?

He tinkers faster now.

China, plates, and cups rattle and clatter around in front of him,
the sounds like nails on chalkboard to my ears.

They crash to the floor, making an island of broken things.

His hands move erratically and he cries to himself.

"I know it's here, I know it's here!"

Without looking back, he throws the dishes behind him. They
nearly hit me. He's going mad, so very, very mad.

He spirals into an unsettling pattern.

Mutter, tinker, throw, mutter.

How many dishes could possibly be in those cabinets?

What is he searching for?

And what will happen when he's done looking…

I wish my feet would move in any direction, but I am stone stiff,
paralyzed at the scene playing out before my eyes.

The fall of a man unknown to me, succumbing to desperation.

His voice grows deeper, chilling my bones.

"I know it's here. I know it's here."

Then he stops tinkering.

His shoulders tense.

He begins to turn to me.

"I know it's here."

THE FILMMAKER

RICKY FENDLER STOOD IN LINE FOR THE TICKET COUNTER. HE was alone, as he most often was these days, and people-watched with his arms folded across his chest. The place felt especially lively today, but that didn't sway him. Ricky was not one to break tradition.

Men and women, young and old, huddled close together as a brisk winter chill swept through the street. Kids from the nearby high school roughhoused, sailors enjoyed their flavor of the week, and all around the conversations buried the silence as they waited in the unusually long line.

Ricky peeked from beneath his hat toward the night sky. It was rather dark, the moon and stars hiding shyly behind every cloud in sight. The only light came from the comforting brights of the cinema, a welcoming glow that had become like a second home to him.

Every Friday since his retirement in '37 he came to the theater, picked up a ticket for the evening show, and watched—or critiqued, rather—the newest blockbuster sensations sweeping the nation. Last week's film had especially irked him, but not for the usual reasons. Ol' Rhett swooned Scarlett and the rest of the audience into a stupor and he hadn't been able to recover since. His doctor blamed his heart, but Ricky knew better. He needed to see it again for himself.

It had been nearly twenty years since he hitchhiked to

Tinseltown, and all he had to show for it were a few flops, a decent backlist, and, in a bold move that nearly bankrupted him, surprise Oscar nominations for best director and best actor with The Filmmaker.

He was certain it was the only reason the studio kept him around or he would've been thrown out to kick rocks with the rest of the rejects years ago. But following his loss, he had been blackballed from making anything like it since, instead subjugated to the writer's rooms of B-list romances that were a far cry from the realities he wanted to project on screen.

He counted the heads of the people in front of him; four left. All were facing Julian in the ticket booth, whose familiar soft tone was carried away with the wind.

Damn that movie.

Ricky cracked his knuckles absentmindedly as he waited, the bitter cold making his skin feel dry and numb. He wondered when was the last time he'd felt smooth skin beneath his hands and not the sandpaper monstrosities time had made them into.

He eyed the woman before him, trembling in a thin, pale blue work dress that did little to warm her skin. He considered giving her his jacket, but she was next in line—it would have been a waste of time and energy. His joints were not what they used to be and neither was his patience.

At least he was sensible enough to bring a coat and hat.

She turned toward him as she shuffled to and fro, her blue eyes narrowing at his brown ones as she clutched her body in a fierce hug. She trailed her eyes over his face and they widened slightly, a look he had nearly forgotten as of late. It made him feel a bit whole again.

"Y-you're the filmmaker?" she asked, her breath coming out in rasps. He could see it clearly shuddering in the foggy light. "Ricky Fendler, right?"

He smiled slowly, a practiced form from his younger, more handsome days. He cocked his head to the side, reciting the all-too-familiar words from his lips. "Depends, are you a fan or a critic?"

The woman chuckled weakly, the trembling perhaps less from the chill and more from her nerves.

"Always a fan, sir. You're a lot tanner than I thought you'd be."

Ricky was no stranger to these comments, but the woman continued, quickly adding, "That film got me through a tough time…"

He wished he could beam with pride like he used to and inquire further about this young woman's life and the reasons his film had been a beacon of hope for her. But instead, he tensed ever so slightly, apprehensively awaiting the words he knew would come next. The way they always did when someone he met brought up The Filmmaker.

He distractedly chewed the inside of his cheek as she took a slight breath to better convey her next, predictable statement.

"…it was robbed at the Oscars, I couldn't believe it!" she continued. "I swear, I never turned off my radio faster…"

He continued to nod, reaching for the pack of cigarettes in his pocket that he'd sworn to the doctor he got rid of weeks ago.

"I don't know how you kept going. I would have set the whole show on fire!" She seemed to forget the cold, moving her hands theatrically as she spoke, no longer hugging her once shivering body. "I don't even remember what that other movie was about."

Ricky smiled politely, flicking his lighter and watching the end of his cigarette turn a bright orange. He took a glorious, soothing puff that made the bitterness dissipate, if only for a moment as the wind picked up and with it a bone-chilling sensation that made his hand tremble awkwardly.

He felt a pain in his chest and dropped the cigarette.

"I hear there's a fire in this picture, too," she continued, "and the man is mighty handsome. Have you seen it?"

Ricky could hear his heart beating in his ears, loud but slow, but she didn't seem to notice his struggle.

"All my friends told me how real it looked…"

He knew the scene she was describing and could picture how masterfully it was shot. A three-strip technicolor camera that made the entire film feel like a painting on screen. He reached down for the cigarette, but it burned weakly on the sidewalk, dying before he could grasp it.

Disappointment was too kind a word for what Ricky felt in that moment, but he couldn't tell if it was because of the cigarette, the heaviness in his chest, or how quickly the woman, much like everyone else, forgot about The Filmmaker.

Ricky took a deep breath and forced himself to straighten. His eyes felt heavy, his glasses fogged. As he made to adjust them, from the corner of his eye in the peripheral often neglected, he saw a shadow lurking by the theater doors. It appeared as a silhouette of a man wearing a heavy, dark coat and top hat, lingering and unmoving. Ricky removed his glasses and it was gone.

"…and wow, I never thought in my day I would see a color picture, but Hollywood's done some fancy stuff lately. I'm sure you know all about it." She nudged him slightly with a wink.

He nodded back feebly, pretending to clean his bifocals to distract himself from the pain inside and the dampness of his eyes. A single tear fell onto the glass and he wiped it away quickly as the woman continued to speak.

Bittersweet were those memories.

The Ambassador Hotel was filled to the brim with celebrities and movie studio executives wearing their best, ready for another

Oscars year. A band was playing their version of hot jazz to entertain the guests and the radio crew was making their final adjustments before the ceremony went live. Ricky stood anxiously behind the stage curtain, fiddling with his cuff link to give his nerves something to focus on. This wasn't his first year in attendance, but it was his first as a presenter. Within the hour he would be on the other side of this red velvet giving the performance of a lifetime.

He fastened and unfastened the top button of his suit, tailor made for him on the studio's dime from a fashion house in the city. It had felt smooth against his skin during the fittings, but now felt too tight, too hot underneath the stage lights. He wasn't savvy about menswear, but the designer made him swear on pain of death to not make any changes when the cameras flashed.

Ricky relented, fastening the button once more.

"You belong here, kid," he whispered to himself. "Act like it."

He looked up in time to see his friend and co-star, David Walters, approaching him.

"Looking dapper, Fendler," David quipped. "I see the ladies have noticed, too." He lifted his chin to a few up-and-coming starlets, who giggled and stared a few feet away.

Ricky smiled back at David, embracing him. "I'm certain they're giving America's Loverboy the eyes."

David flashed the group a smile and Ricky saw first-hand the meaning of making women swoon. David was in style, and he knew it—all dark hair, green eyes, and tall figure. He'd become a breakout actor two years ago after starring in Suns over Sevilla and was a studio favorite. It was a miracle he had enough time in his schedule to co-star in The Filmmaker, but no one else could have done it better.

"I have a good feeling about tonight," David mused, taking in all the lights, the assistants running to and fro, and the unfettered chaos of behind-the-scenes action. He pulled the curtain to the side ever so slightly, peeking out at the stars shining from their seats.

"I hope so." Ricky let out a shaky breath. There was a lot riding on tonight's success.

David closed the curtain. "They'd be mad not to give it to you." He patted Ricky on the back. "You're a hotshot, Fendler, and everyone here knows it."

Ricky met David's eyes. They were sincere, genuine. He wanted to believe it was true, that someone like him could truly make it.

"Just wait, you'll see" David continued. "I'll be up on stage, open the envelope slowly to build anticipation, act like I'm utterly shocked when I see the letter inside, and then announce The Filmmaker! Made by the one and only Ricky Fendler!"

Ricky Fendler.

"Hey, Mr. Fendler!"

The two men turned to the voice. It was one of the hotel's security guards.

"Yes?" Ricky responded.

"There's a woman here, claims she knows you and won't leave," the guard explained. "Do you know a Thalia?"

"Thalia?" David asked.

Ricky felt his heart stop.

"...I ran out of work to come here. I didn't care if I was alone. It's all anyone can talk about—the romance, the dalliances!"

Ricky wasn't sure how long the young woman had been speaking, but darkness encroached on his vision.

Thump.

Thump.

Thump.

"And oh, how could I forget that English actress. My friend auditioned for the role of Scarlett and lost it to her. She was pea green with envy when she found out!"

Ricky pinched the bridge of his nose, trying to stay upright while the world spun around him. From the corner of his eye, he saw a shadow lingering behind the ticket booth.

"...but my father always says, the devil is in the details. Boy was he right."

Ricky tried to raise his hand to point at the shadow, but its weight was too heavy now. The shadow was growing closer, and the young woman's voice faded into the distance as he gripped his aching chest.

Was it the memories?

Was it the sound of grief finally overtaking him?

Was it…

"Sir? Sir! If you could step up, please, we are on a tight schedule."

Ricky lifted his head. The people around him, the woman, were gone. It was only him and a ticketer outside.

"W-where did everyone go?"

The ticketer smiled from his booth, almost pitifully. "They left you behind, but not to worry—I saved you a seat." He raised a hand, the off-white ticket stub resting between his fingers. The shadow, too, was gone.

"Er—sorry." Ricky shuffled to him.

You're an old man, Ricky, getting older every day.

"Where is Julian?" Ricky asked, handing the ticketer a quarter.

Under the dim yellow light of the booth, this boy looked familiar, but Ricky couldn't place him. The ticketer's blond hair was cropped into a fashionable combover like Ricky once had when he cared about such things. His freckled face and dimpled cheeks made him appear much younger than he probably was.

The ticketer took the coin and smiled. He couldn't have been older than sixteen and met Ricky's gaze with hazel eyes that seemed to stare right through him. "Julian's not here yet."

"He was just here," Ricky mumbled, taking the ticket. "In all my years of coming here, he's never left a Friday shift early."

"Julian is on time, I assure you, sir."

Ricky thought to quip back at the ticketer, but something in his tone and Ricky's unwillingness to meet his too-attentive stare kept him silent.

The ticketer handed him the stub. "Enjoy. It's a packed house tonight, Mr. Fendler."

Ricky nodded. He was taking a step toward the door when the ticketer called out again.

"The Filmmaker should've won. We get a lot of requests for it here."

Ricky stilled. He turned back to the ticketer, but the booth was gone. The only thing remaining was the theater door and himself.

Suddenly, he now wanted to watch the windy film instead of being outside feeling this uncomfortable chill in his bones. He had the unsettling feeling of being watched, that something or someone was close behind him, beckoning him to turn and face it. Ricky grasped the brass handle of the door, cool beneath his fingertips, and pulled.

The inside of the theater was nothing like he remembered. The wood-paneled walls had been replaced with golden trim and extravagant decor—palm trees, chandeliers, and ice sculptures lined the expansive room. Tables were fitted with white cloth and colorful chairs filled with people in their finest suits and gowns crowded the space. Ricky's eyes widened as the realization dawned on him.

This was Cocoanut Grove.

In the Ambassador Hotel.

One of the staff, a man dressed decadently in a white suit, approached him. "Right this way, Mr. Fendler. We've been waiting for you."

"Me?" Ricky asked as the man helped him remove a homburg and fancy topcoat.

"Yes. You are the filmmaker, after all," the man replied with a gentle smile, taking the hat and coat and handing it to another one of the staff who quickly carried it away. He brushed a piece of lint off of Ricky's three-piece suit, inspecting him.

"Now you're ready for the show." He smiled kindly and turned on his heel, motioning for Ricky to follow.

Ricky did, confused, as the man led him between tables.

"Wait," Ricky said, "I prefer to sit at—"

"The back," the man finished for him. "Yes, we know."

He led Ricky to the only empty table in the otherwise packed room.

"Why is no one else sitting here?" Ricky demanded. "I thought I got the last ticket?"

"Because you are the filmmaker," the man repeated, placing his hands to his sides uniformly.

His stare was attentive, yet hollow. Ricky couldn't quite

describe why it made him feel so unnerved.

"Can I get you anything before the show begins?"

Ricky looked around. The audience was eerily silent and faced the white screen on the stage before them, waiting for the show to begin.

"No, thank you."

The man nodded and leaned in close. "The Filmmaker was the clear winner, sir. I hope you don't mind me saying."

Ricky stood, confused.

"Apologies, I should have introduced myself. My name is Samuel, and I am your companion this evening." Samuel pulled out Ricky's seat for him. "We find that it comforts our guests to have a friend."

Ricky sat again, slowly, taking in the space.

He loved to sit in the back of any event, but especially when watching films. He loved to see how the people around him truly felt about the scenes unfolding before their eyes. The shock and awe, the heartbreak and tears—he loved it all. He was never alone when he was amid the audience.

But now, at this table in this large room, he felt rather isolated. As if he shouldn't be here. Even with Samuel, who took the seat next to him.

Ricky took a closer look at the audience once more. Their eyes were glued to the front, their attention never wavering to speak or even breathe, it seemed. They were like puppets or statues filling the space with nothing but caricatured features. Ricky considered leaving, and had just begun mumbling his apologies when a middle-aged man with bright pink cheeks and a broad smile took center stage.

"Good evening, ladies and gentlemen!" he bellowed, though

it was rather unnecessary. "I am your humble host, George, here to make an announcement. Tonight we have a special guest. Our one and only The Filmmaker!"

Ricky didn't have time to think about this declaration before a resounding, earth-shattering applause erupted. His heart leapt from his chest and he nearly stumbled out of his chair. All around him the audience clapped with unnatural grins plastered on their faces, their emotionless eyes bearing down on him.

"Why do they look like that?" Ricky managed through winded breath.

Samuel helped him back into his seat. "They are our guests, sir. No need to worry yourself."

"Guests?"

The applause died down, the audience sat in silence once more, and George continued. "Tonight, we have lined up an exceptional showing! It is our sincere hope that it entertains, moves, and even inspires you all. And remember, love it or hate it, make sure we can hear it."

The host bowed deeply and then silence fell once more along with the lights. It was dark for a brief, unsettling moment before the screen flashed the familiar countdown.

"What are you doing here?" Ricky demanded, closing the door to the supply closet. He was down a hundred bucks after paying off the security guard in exchange for his silence, and now he was in a foul mood.

"Is that how you talk to your sister? After all these years?!"

"Shhh, not so loud!" Ricky hushed.

"You never answered my letters, Enrique."

96

"Don't call me that."

"Oh, that's right—you're Ricky now, aren't you?"

"It's just a name."

"Is that what you tell yourself? What would Mami think?"

Ricky paced as much as he could in the cramped closet, running his fingers through his hair. "What do you want? Money? A job?"

Thalia cast her eyes to the floor. "I'm in trouble."

Ricky closed his own. "How much trouble?"

"He's dead, Ricky."

"Who?"

"You know who."

Ricky grabbed his sister by the shoulders. "Please, please tell me you're lying."

Thalia faced him, tears falling from her swollen eyes. "I have him in the trunk of my car. I need to get out of here before the cops find me."

"No." Ricky pushed her away. "No, no, no, not now. Not ever. I left this all behind me, I'm a new man now."

"A new man?" Thalia spat angrily. "You sold yourself to these men in suits the same way you did to those filling up their tubs with moonshine."

"This is different!"

"Hell, you even look like one of them. How much dye did it take to make your hair so light?" She reached her fingers up to touch it, but Ricky turned his head away.

"Dammit, Thalia. I can't help you. I won't help you."

"You don't have a choice. If it wasn't for me, you'd never be here."

"I did this on my own!"

97

"I stayed behind to keep them from beating you to death while you jumped on the first bus out of town!"

"This could ruin me!"

"See, that's your damn problem. You think the world revolves around you."

Ricky pointed a finger at her. "I wanted to do something with my life besides begging for scraps—"

"And you think that's what we wanted?"

"It's your damn fault for not trying to be better!"

Thalia's eyes widened, her mouth going slack. Ricky's hear raced. He had not seen his sister in years, nor any of his other family—not since he ran away from their small farming town. He wanted to see the beach, to find a city and meet a nice girl. To get away from the men who lurked in dark corners promising quick cash for little favors.

"I didn't have a choice. Do you think I would have come here if I did?"

"Who else knows?"

"No one."

"Thalia, don't lie to me."

She bit her lip. "I don't think anyone else knows. I just need a little help before they find me. Please."

Ricky rubbed his eyes. He couldn't believe that after years of running, his old life could come crashing back like this. "I'll give you whatever cash I have in my pocket, but that's all I have. I used everything else on this." He gestured to his new look as if it somehow signified what he meant.

"I understand," she breathed.

He pulled out a few bills and handed them to her. Shame wracked him. Thinking his absence would make their lives easier was nothing but a childish wish.

Thalia took the money carefully in her hands, not counting a single bill as she placed the wad in her purse. "Thank you."

She wrapped her arms around his waist the way she would when they were kids. Ricky hugged her back. In his arms his little sister reminded him of the good parts of home, but also the guilt he carried leaving her behind. She let go and he stood motionless as she moved past him to the door.

"I'm proud of you," she whispered. "One of us finally made it."

Ricky nodded slowly, his jaw tensing, trying to keep himself composed.

"You might be Ricky to these men," Thalia whispered, "but you will always be Enrique. Don't let them take that from you, too."

~~~~

"I-I don't understand," Ricky stuttered, watching the memory of his past play out on screen. "Why are we watching this?"

"You're The Filmmaker," Samuel whispered.

"What does that mean? Why does everyone keep calling me that?"

"Because it's who you are."

"I'm not a filmmaker anymore. That was just a one-hit wonder. I never made anything like it again."

Samuel nodded, his eyes turning to Ricky. "I would argue this is better, isn't it?"

Ricky fixed his eyes on the screen and watched as his sister left the closet and hurried down the hall to the exit, passing David on her way out. He stopped her and they had an exchange. He handed her a slip of paper.

"I never got to tell her how sorry I was…for leaving her. For abandoning her when she needed me most."

Samuel nodded patiently. "It is human to err."

"Yes, but…"

"It was not your fault," Samuel finished.

Ricky turned back to the screen. His sister jumped in her beaten-up car and pulled away from the hotel. As she turned right onto Wilshire Boulevard, he noticed something strange on the screen. A shadow, like that of a man, lingered on the side of the street. The clip cut to black.

"What was that?!" Ricky demanded.

"Shh," Samuel hushed, "you don't want to upset your guests."

Ricky looked around the room. Everyone was now staring at him.

"B-but the shadowman—it was there, I saw it."

"Yes, you did."

"I thought it was my imagination, I thought—" Ricky turned about the room nervously. "What if it's here? What if it's coming for me?" The eyes of the audience never wavered from him as panic clawed its way through his body.

"How do I get them to stop?" he begged.

"By watching what happens next."

The microphones were on, the stage was set, and all Ricky had to do was read from the cue cards positioned just past the stage. They were large white poster boards, the words written in bold black letters. His heart thundered in his chest, beads of sweat pricked at his temples, and the crowd roared with applause.

No sooner had his sister left than he was whisked away onto

the stage, with barely a moment to think about her parting words. They consumed him, eating away at the near perfect facade he had crafted over so many years.

Enrique.

He swallowed, kissing his co-presenter Sandra on both cheeks and trying to smile graciously to the audience. She was grinning from ear to ear, and turned to the audience, ready to speak. Ever the professional.

"Good evening, America! Welcome to the Oscars. My name is Sandra Fallis, star of The Never Men…" A thunderous applause greeted her and she gestured to Ricky.

Enrique.

He saw the cards, the words in bold lettering: *…and I am Ricky Fendler, star and director of The Filmmaker!*

But he couldn't say it. He couldn't do it.

Not the way they wanted him to.

Years later, he would blame the tension of the moment, his sister for nearly dropping a dead man at his door, the shame he felt for hiding who he really was.

…you will always be Enrique. Don't let them take that from you, too.

"And I am Enrique Fernando, director and star of The Filmmaker!"

He smiled broadly for the newspaper cameras, but the crowd was less enthused. A few clapped, but otherwise it was silent. Members of the audience exchanged confused looks.

Sandra put on the performance of a lifetime, quickly continuing with the cards, and together they did their bit, pretending as if nothing went wrong.

They walked out stage right for the next presenters, smiling and waving to the crowd as they went. No sooner were they covered by the thick curtain than Sandra whipped around to face him.

"What the hell was that, Ricky?! This was my big shot and you ruined it!"

Ricky swallowed. "My name is Enrique."

"And my real name is Francine, but we all have a goddamn part to play. I swear to god, if you ruined anything with the studio heads for me, I'll hunt down every *barrio* I can find and make you wish you were never born!"

Ricky watched the screen as Sandra turned away down the long hall.

The scene was set to end—Ricky could feel it in his bones. But instead, the camera lingered on Sandra walking through the crowded back stage, further and further from the camera's unmoving gaze. Ricky's eyes took in the scene. The people moved about hurriedly, no one paying much attention to the man who fumbled on a live broadcast, all with their own marks to meet. He nearly asked Samuel if the clip was broken, but the words never left his tongue.

His eyes widened, tears forming at the corners as he saw it.

Closer now, the shadowman lingered in the long shot, peeking out from the supply closet.

"It's coming for me!" Ricky stood, looking for the nearest escape.

"We are only watching what you want us to," Samuel said, calmly.

"No! I don't know what twisted game you have going here, but I'm done. Take me back home."

Samuel stared. "You are home."

"This isn't home. You've brought me here to make a mockery of me! That thing is coming to get me!"

"I didn't bring you anywhere," Samuel said calmly. "You came here all on your own."

"Like hell I did!"

"Hush now," Samuel urged, "you will upset your guests."

The crowd turned to face him once more as the scene finally shifted to Ricky being confronted by the studio heads. He remembered too well the feeling of regret, of heartache, of foolishness. But in this shot, the shadowman was nowhere to be seen.

Ricky averted his eyes, turning to Samuel.

"I just wanted the world to know it was me...that I was the filmmaker. Not them."

"And so you did."

"But look what happened. I'm here now! Sitting in front of a hundred ghosts and watching my wretched past while something waits for me." Ricky felt the weight on his shoulders. He placed his hands on the table to keep from falling to his knees. "It's waiting for my show to end."

Samuel didn't answer. Instead, he patted the seat next to him.

It was a montage.

Ricky lost the Oscar that night.

And all the movie deals that had been promised to him vanished into thin air.

For the next couple of years, he wrote under his pseudonym in the studio writer's room. His affinity for writing hits was without question, but he was ignored at most meetings, only called upon to churn out B-list films to fill the theater quotas.

He neglected to dye his hair anymore, and its natural color returned in swaths of wavy black against the blondish hues that still fought for purchase on his scalp. Sometimes he would run his fingers through the strands and remember what Thalia said about it.

Ricky never did hear about any murder in the newspaper, and he hoped that Thalia was finally free at last. He pictured his sister in some faraway city discovering herself, just as he had. Perhaps she was a starlet in the local theater, maybe even singing blues in a club somewhere, but more than anything, he hoped she was safe. He even hoped they would one day meet again.

He was the last to leave the office most nights, finding comfort in the solitude and lack of wary gazes around him. On one such night, Ricky collected his blazer and put out his cigarette. His latest romance about a woman lost in the jungles of Nicaragua and saved by an archeologist was freshly deposited on his boss's desk.

It wasn't his best work, but it was something that had made the past few days entertaining for once.

The office phone rang, and Ricky picked it up.

"Ricky here."

"Ricky, I'm glad I got you. It's me, David."

Ricky nearly dropped the phone. He couldn't think of what to say. He hadn't seen David since that very night his costar had announced *Cars and Alley Cats* the winner of Best Picture at the Oscars. The studio peeled David and every A- and B-list celebrity from Ricky's side, the backlash for associating with the Latino kid swift and painful.

"Ricky? Ricky, are you there?"

Ricky cleared his throat. "Yes, what do you want, David? It's late."

"I'm only in Hollywood for the night. I'm heading out to Spain tomorrow."

The sequel to Suns over Sevilla was all anyone had talked about for the last week. The studio was expected to pay big money for it. A guaranteed box office hit.

"Good for you, David," Ricky mumbled.

"I wanted to get something off my chest. Do you have time for coffee?"

"It's near midnight."

"Even better."

Ricky drove faster than usual to the bar. It was settled on the outskirts of the city near a train station. It was no secret that David didn't want to be seen with him. He, too, was on thin ice after a recent scandal broke about David's affair with some woman the studio didn't approve of. He was meant to be a bachelor—anything else would harm his image and therefore their ticket sales. It always came down to money.

He entered the bar, where David was seated at the far end, barely visible in the faint light. He looked disheveled, his five o'clock shadow scraggled and patchy, his eyes red. He was hollow. This was not the David he remembered. This was someone who had seen things that kept him up at night.

Ricky approached him and David cut to the chase.

"The envelope."

"Envelope?" Ricky asked, taking his seat.

"The Oscars. Our Oscars. That envelope."

Ricky shook his head. "Why am I here, David?"

David chugged the rest of his drink. "When I opened it, the

letter inside was blank. It didn't even feel like the cards I've read off in the past—it was just a thin sheet of paper that someone must've thrown in there."

"I don't understand."

"I don't have a lot of time, so let me finish." He pushed his glass aside and stared at Ricky with glazed, green eyes. "The cue cards, however, were raised and waiting for me. In all my years of presenting, I never once had to read the winner from a cue card."

"What are you saying—"

"You won, Ricky. The Filmmaker was the real winner that night."

"No…"

"It's true. I found out at an after party that one of the studio heads ordered the change moments before I was handed the envelope. They barely wrote the winner on the cue cards in time for me to read it live on the radio."

"Why?"

"You know why." David took out his wallet. "There was no way they'd let someone like you, the real you, win against someone like them."

"Why are you telling me this?"

David took out a bill and placed it on the table. "Because you deserve to know the truth."

"Bullshit. You would have told me years ago."

David leaned closer. "I was wrong. I'm sorry."

"You're not sorry, you just finally got a taste of being on their crap list and now you've come looking for sympathy." Ricky stood, taking a few steps away from him when David spoke.

"Thalia says she wants to see you."

"Turn it off! Turn the whole damn thing off!" Ricky shouted, throwing a centerpiece toward the screen. He was too far back for it to matter much, and it landed with a pathetic thump before the stage.

"This seems to upset you."

"Of course it does!" Ricky pounded his fist against the table.

A scene of him shoving David against the wall, hands fisting his collar and ready to give him the beating of his lifetime, was on full display.

"But you're the filmmaker."

"Stop calling me that!" he shouted. Ricky swiveled around and saw the eyes of his guests, large and unnatural, staring at him from their seats. Their statuesque bodies were limp beneath the decadent, rich fabrics of their attire. "I'm not The Filmmaker!" he shouted to them. "I lost, I lost, I lost it all, and for what?!"

He gestured to the screen, which showed him loosening his grip on David as the actor explained everything. The camera panned out from an overhead shot, showing their interaction as both tense and desperate. And there, as the camera was still for a beat, before the clip would predictably turn black, there was the shadowman, standing a few feet behind Ricky, its arm outstretched as if to touch him.

Ricky didn't want to be here anymore. He turned around, searching for the exit, but there was none there. The entire room seemed to yawn and stretch for miles full of screens and stages and tables and guests. "Get me out of here! Get me out of here before it gets me!"

Ricky shouted to Samuel.

But Samuel did not budge.

Even as Ricky flipped the table over, Samuel did not move from his chair.

"You did not kill her, Ricky."

Ricky heaved, tears falling from his weary eyes. "Yes, I did."

"You didn't kill her," Samuel repeated calmly.

Ricky's legs buckled and he fell to his knees.

"But I did. I did."

Ricky drove faster than he ever had before. The car cruised at a high fifty, pushing the limits of his Model T. In the night, the roads were empty and the lights were sparse, but he followed the directions David had written on the bar napkin.

Soon, he was back in Los Angeles, racing to the hotel his sister was hiding out in. David swore he loved Thalia, had rejected nearly every offer and threat from the studio to run away with her. But they found him before he left the city and now the studio's fixers were looking for her—the woman who threatened their next big payout.

Ricky knocked on the door.

But there was no answer.

He knocked harder, looking left and right to make sure he wasn't followed.

"Thalia, it's me. It's Enrique."

No answer.

His nerves were getting the best of him. Any second, he felt like he would see the studio's fixers turning a corner and racing toward him.

What if the streets weren't that empty?

What if they'd seen him driving from the bar?

What if...

He took a few steps back and kicked the door down.

He sprinted into the room, ready to whisk his sister away before they were sure to come. He would explain everything later. He would take her away from here. He would right his wrongs—

But then he saw her.

Thalia was sprawled out on the bed, a bottle of pills in her hand.

Enrique watched as he became a wretched, broken man on screen.

And the shadowman stood close behind him. It was no longer trying to hide off camera, no longer trying to lurk in the dark. It was the dark, and it clung to him.

The camera panned out as the tragic scene unfolded.

Then the screen faded to black.

The lights of the room brightened.

"The fixer who did it was a cousin of the man who beat her," Enrique managed, not bothering to wipe the tears from his eyes. They traveled slowly down his cheeks, taking their time to make their presence known.

"The one she killed," Samuel said. It was not a question.

"Yes."

"I see."

Enrique turned to Samuel. "She was trying to start a new life. Had met David that night at the Oscars. They kept in touch and he fell in love with her."

Samuel said nothing; he simply listened.

"David couldn't live with himself after that. He took his life on set in Spain and they never did finish Suns over Sevilla. I like to think that it was his last 'fuck you' to the studio. It's the only way I can sleep better at night."

"I hope you meet them again."

"I do, too." When Enrique met Samuel's eyes, he could see himself within them. A crestfallen, broken thing looked back.

"We wait to see what your guests think."

"What do you mean?"

"You want them to clap."

"Clap?"

"Yes."

"And if they don't?"

Samuel gestured to stage right. "Then it's waiting for you."

Enrique followed his eyes, and there, lingering just behind the curtain, was the shadowman.

"I don't want to go with him."

"I'm afraid I can't stop it."

Enrique's lip trembled.

"And if they clap?"

"Then you can leave."

"And go where?"

"Home."

George walked on stage, his pink cheeks even brighter now, and the smile on his face even wider. He seemed completely oblivious to the shadowman as he addressed the audience. "Ladies and gentlemen, The Filmmaker!"

Enrique turned to Samuel. "Thank you. For being with me."

Enrique stood slowly, loosening his necktie just enough to swallow the lump in his throat.

The audience stayed quiet. Their eyes followed him as he moved through the sea of tables. A walk that at one time in his life he would have cherished, maybe even died for. He walked up the steps, imagining they were those of that Oscars night all those years ago. That it could have been him, a poor boy from nowhere, going to accept the golden statue against all odds.

His name—his real name—would be engraved on it, and he would tell all his children and grandchildren about it. He would plant the seeds of dreams in their heads and make sure they knew that someone like them, too, could make it.

George shook his hand and left Enrique alone on the stage.

Enrique faced the audience, the spotlight bright and nearly blinding, obscuring their faces. He could feel the shadowman inching toward him. It was too quiet in this room and on this stage.

Enrique patted the beads of sweat on his forehead with a handkerchief from his breast pocket.

He thought about his life.

His decisions.

His isolation.

The shadowman's fingertips reached out to touch him.

Enrique closed his eyes, understanding his fate.

Then there was the smallest clap.

So faint he could barely hear it over the pounding of his heart.

Or was it his imagination…

FORTY MINUTES

"DRIVING THROUGH THE DESERT ISN'T FOR THE FAINT-HEARTED."

I say this to cheer myself up, but I can now see my cold breath in front of me as the frigid winter chill creeps into my car. I curse my broken heater, wishing I had replaced it last summer when I had the money.

The last rays of sunlight fall victim to the blue-black hues of night in my rearview mirror. But instead of feeling better, I clench my hands tighter on the steering wheel, trying to ignore the blanket of darkness falling around me. The rolling hills and snowy cacti that spotted the vast, empty lands before are now faint outlines in the distance.

I think of everything that could be hiding, or coming out of hiding, in the dark. When my eyes shift to the directions on my phone, my heart stutters. There's another hour left of my drive. My hands feel clammy and I wipe my palms on my jeans, one at a time, before resuming my grip on the wheel.

"You should have left earlier, dammit."

The night sky swallows up all that can be seen until there is nothing but my headlights to keep me sane. Not even a star takes pity on me, preferring its seclusion to lighting my way home. I can hear the car as it pierces through the gusty wind, the engine sputtering along the straight, narrow highway with not a single car in sight.

My mind trails to all the true crime shows I wish I could scrub from my memory now. The images permeate my mind, taking root—video clips of accidents left undiscovered until a curious passerby decided to investigate, and surveillance footage of bodies found in the middle of nowhere.

I push my foot further down on the accelerator, not too fast but enough to earn me a ticket should a cop be sitting idly off the road. Part of me would welcome that if it meant knowing I wasn't driving a highway devoid of other people. That thought is fleeting as I recall one case states away where men used old police vehicles to stop innocent only imagine what someone like that would do to me.

"There's nothing to be scared of," I scold myself. "Stop it."

Still, my breath is shaky and visible as I release my foot from the gas and set cruise control to a safe five miles per hour above the speed limit. I sneak another glance at my phone. Fifty-two minutes left. A lump forms in my throat and I pick it up to double check the time again.

Fifty-two minutes left.

I place it back in the cup holder as dread begins to claw up my spine. My hands are trembling, my lips are chapped, but none of that seems to matter as much as the thought of having to spend nearly an hour in this isolating desert.

My eyes strain against the dark. Even with my high beams on, I can only see a short distance ahead. Snow begins to fall and I can practically feel the road getting slicker beneath my tires. The wind howls against my vehicle as if my mere presence has set off its angry tirade, like a collection of ancestral voices cursing me for intruding upon their peace.

I reach for my phone, set to play any kind of music that will drown out the groans of the wind and distract me, but there's no signal. I chew on my lip nervously and place the phone down again.

Fifty minutes left.

The snow picks up and I turn on my windshield wipers to clear my view, leaning forward as if that would help me see any better. I feel the tension rising, thinking of all the scenarios that could go wrong in a fifty-minute drive the way women always do before they walk out to their cars, when they cross an unfamiliar street, or even when they're driving alone in the dark.

If I were to get into an accident, how long would it take for someone to find me?

The wind is roaring now, trying to push my car off the road, but my fierce grip on the wheel keeps me moving straight ahead. The leather binding surely imprints on my skin as I squeeze it tighter.

Would I make it long out in the cold?

The snow pounds like my heart against my windshield and I turn the wipers to full speed. Too quickly, the snow is turning to ice on the glass. I flip on my defroster, hoping against hope that it will work just this once.

Who would find me?

My defroster is doing nothing but sputtering cold air into my frozen space and I turn it off, frustrated. Tears prick at the corners of my eyes as I wipe the inside of the windshield with my sleeve, desperate to clear any bit of my view.

No matter how much sense it would make, I don't want to pull over to use my ice scraper and give the monsters lurking in the dark a chance to seize me. Because though I know it's near impossible, and that creatures only exist in scary stories told at slumber parties, my imagination is running fervent and wild. The horrors have taken hold of my mind, sinking their long, sharp claws deeper inside, prevailing over sound logic. Every inch of darkness hides something sinister in its depths, waiting for the opportunity to strike. Every roar of the wind is something pursuing me. I shift my eyes suddenly to my phone.

Forty minutes left.

My hand trembles so violently that as I hastily retrieve it from the glass, I shove my elbow against the gear shift. The old car immediately sputters and whines. The icy grip of panic seizes me as I struggle to force the gear back into drive. The car swerves on the slick road, and I jerk the steering wheel and press the brake to prevent it from toppling into a ditch off the highway. It skids to a stop and I barely have enough time to take a breath before I see headlights approaching.

"Fuck!"

I push the accelerator just in time for the car to pass. It barely misses me as it honks angrily away through the deluge of snow and ice, its lights disappearing into the dark.

I sit in my freezing car, lingering in drive on the right side of the road, taking deep, gulping breaths as my heart fumbles between my throat and my chest. My hands are still in a white-knuckled grip on the steering wheel, as if letting them go would mean certain death. The wind growls at me, a low moan that's even more threatening than its howling before. I squeeze my eyes shut and beg it to stop. I swear to anything that exists that I will never drive in the desert this late again if I can just make it through this.

The car and everything outside become silent. Unwelcome dread pricks at me once more as adrenaline spikes through my veins. I turn my head slowly, peering down at my phone lying motionless in the cup holder.

Forty minutes left.

My pulse quickens, my mouth is dry, and I can't escape the feeling that something is very wrong. But I can't stay here—staying here means something, or someone, will find me.

I force my foot down as gently as I can on the accelerator, and my car miraculously whirs into motion. When I look out my windshield, the snow has disappeared, the tires no longer making that wet sound along the highway. The wind which consumed me so ferociously only moments before has died down into nothing particularly discernable. I notice the stars begin to shine in the sky, lighting the desert around me, illuminating clusters of cacti and tumbleweeds as far as the darkness will allow me to see.

I loosen my grip on the steering wheel, noticing the city lights in the distance. Any remaining tension thaws when I see how it sparkles just beyond the crest of the hill ahead. Without realizing it, I'm sobbing tears of sweet relief. Home is so close I can reach out and touch it.

The lights are shining brighter now than I remember, and I glance down at my phone.

Forty minutes left.

"There's no way," I murmur incredulously.

I wipe my tears with my fingertips, noticing how warm my touch is. My eyes trail from my phone to the broken heater.

My heart sinks.

And the lights shine brighter than ever.

When did it start working?

GNOMES

Irene never considered herself gifted in the garden.

In her eighty-two years of life, her thumb never showed a hint of green. She thought about this as she stared at the unkempt shrubs through her kitchen window.

The garden had not felt human hands since the death of her husband, Hugh, six months ago. And besides, these were his shrubs, not hers. She'd wanted hydrangeas and he brought back hebes, planted them while she was out on errands, and told her to be fine with it when she returned.

She huffed at the memory, a bitter taste in her mouth. For Irene's part, she would have rather ordered the lot of them torn apart and burned in the backyard. But the thought of her grown children chastising her for ridding herself of their father's handiwork so soon after his death kept her from tossing a gallon of gasoline on the wretched, poky things.

Irene squinted behind her glasses, trying to discern how much effort it would take for her to trim them herself. They grew rather wildly, as if they were having a tantrum beneath the wet skies of Seattle's finest autumn clouds.

She leaned closer to the window, peeking up to see how long it would be until she could venture outdoors unbothered, then rolled her eyes.

"I hate the rain," she muttered.

She began to fiddle with the blinds, tugging at an angle to make them fall back into place on the windowsill, when she heard laughter.

Her dead husband's laughter.

sound toward the window. And there, in the far corner of the backyard, she saw the strangest little garden gnome.

How on earth did I miss this?

It was round and quite unappealing, the ceramic figure covered in chipped blue paint. Its pointed cap was missing the tip a faded gray showing through where it should have ended in blue like the rest of the gnome's clothing. She couldn't see much else from inside her house, but its long white beard stood out, reminding her of him. Nearly two years ago, Hugh had insisted that his shaving days were over and began to let his strands grow like the shrubs.

Irene narrowed her eyes at the vile creature, her fear subsiding to rage. She hated gnomes and her husband knew she hated them, too. They were creepy, small, and perpetually cheery, even when the rain soaked their bodies and chipped away at their colorful exterior. She thought she had rid herself of all of them weeks ago, but apparently this one survived.

No, this would not do.

She pursed her lips as she released the blinds, not caring if they settled correctly on the windowsill.

Irene grabbed a shovel from the garage, determined to smash the figure to pieces with whatever strength she had. She couldn't explain why she was so angry, only that she was and that this gnome was the final straw. She lifted the hood on her poncho and peered over at the neighbor's house as the rain tapped against her body.

It was owned by a young couple who used to keep to themselves, but seemed too curious about what she did as of late. Asking her questions, prying as to her whereabouts. And more than once she would catch them lingering too long at their back door, watching her.

Their porch lights were on, but no one seemed to notice as she crept to the gnome, walking along the fence line as if she were a predator stalking her prey. She didn't want to let him know that she was coming for him.

Every day it was something since her husband's passing—a

pile of his dirty laundry stuffed under the bed, shoes tossed around the house, chores found undone that he'd promised to tend to before he passed.

Irene could hear the gnome laughing like Hugh used to. She was always the butt of his jokes, and now he continued to insult her from beyond the grave with this wretched thing, and a broken one at that.

It had to go. Just like the rest of them.

She approached it, noticing how disheveled and cracked it actually was. The blue was not new, but a faded hue diluted from the elements. It was no longer smiling but appeared…frightened.

"Don't look at me like that," she spat. "This is Hugh's fault, not mine. Getting whatever he wanted and leaving me with the mess."

The gnome didn't respond, not that she expected it to. It remained still with its ugly exterior and droopy green eyes. It would be like Hugh to get something like this and not tell her, something that looked just like him to irk her. She wondered if he'd painted it himself.

No wonder it looked so ugly.

She raised the shovel, her arms shaking with the weight, and was set to throw it down at the concrete creature when a voice called out.

"Mrs. Delano! What're you doing out here? It's raining."

That damn neighbor.

Startled, Irene dropped the shovel behind her, and shouted back, "Mind your business! I'm getting rid of the gnome."

She narrowed her eyes at the man who raised a bewildered brow. His wife stood just inside the back door and handed him a jacket, trying to not meet Irene's gaze. The man took it and shrugged it on, heading off his back porch and toward Irene. The chain link fence hid nothing between them.

"Mrs. Delano, I told you, call me Isaac." He met her wary gaze. "Now, you shouldn't be outside in this weather—you'll get sick. I can help you tend to the garden when it clears up."

Something about his tone and mere presence irked her. She curled her lip.

"Are your ears broken? This is between me and the gnome."

She pointed to where the gnome stood, all blue ceramic and chipped markings, vexing her.

Its green eyes appeared to stare at her from beneath its cone hat, so lifelike she felt as if she were staring at her husband. She wished she was strong enough to break it with her bare hands. She could've been done with it by now.

Isaac's eyes moved to where Irene pointed and then back to his wife peeking through the ajar door of their house. He scratched the back of his head and let out a deep sigh.

"I think this can wait, don't you? I've helped you get rid of a few this week alone."

"No, it can't!"

He rubbed his eyes. "Perhaps you should visit your sons for the week. I can get rid of the gnome while you're gone."

"Gone?! What are you saying?"

Isaac turned back to his wife, shrugging, and as if that communicated something between them, she disappeared into their house. He turned back to Irene. "Let me walk you back inside."

Before Irene could protest, Isaac opened the gate between their fences.

"I don't need any help, I just want to get rid of the gnome!" she spat, bending to pick up the shovel. Isaac got to it before she could.

"It's time to go back inside, Mrs. Delano. I'll take care of it for you."

The audacity of this man. Irene thought about cursing him out, but as she whipped her head to face him, she realized how dark it was outside.

Their suburban paradise twinkled with porch lights, but otherwise, even with gentle rain, it was nearly pitch black. As if the lights were nothing more than sparse yellow paint flecks on black canvas. She wiped the rain from her face.

How on earth?

Isaac gestured gently to the back door, shovel in hand. Irene protested and cursed him every step of the way, but even so, he continued along calmly. As Isaac opened the door for her, Irene turned to the backyard once more.

That gnome stared back at her, its mouth twisted in laughter.

"Mom, I don't understand you anymore."

It was a day later and her sons, Benny and Chris, had driven from Tacoma. Irene had not slept, the laughter creeping in through the darkness, mocking her. But when she would peek through the kitchen window, over the tangled shrubs and out toward the edge of the backyard, the gnome was no longer there.

Her sons sat across from her at the small kitchen table. She could barely hear them over the sound of laughter and the rain tapping against the glass. It felt like hammers on her skull...

"You need someone to be with you. Clearly you aren't doing well with dad gone and we're all just worried about you," Benny, her eldest, continued.

Tap.

Tap.

Tap.

She took a sip of her coffee and nearly spit it out as it passed her lips. It tasted bitter and rotten. When Irene looked inside the mug, the coffee was a deep red.

"What is this?"

Benny sighed, rubbing his temples with his fingers. "You need to lay off the sugar, Mom. Have you not been listening to Dr. Amos? See, this is what I'm talking about." He turned to Chris, who shook his head slowly, but remained silent.

Irene couldn't understand what was wrong with them. What on earth possessed them to give her something like this? It was like they were turning into their father more and more each day.

Tap.

Laugh.

Tap.

Laugh.

"I wish that damn rain would stop!" she huffed, rubbing her tired eyes. "And the laughing. Oh, that laugh."

"Mom, what are you—" Chris began, but Benny placed a hand on his shoulder, silencing him.

"Robert and I talked it over, and we would love it if you came to live with us. You would always be taken care of and you wouldn't have to be so alone," Benny said, reaching for her hand.

She pulled back and stood, taking the coffee cup with her.

This would not do.

"Mom, didn't you hear me?" Benny furrowed his brow.

Irene walked over to the sink, dumping the coffee into it.

Tap.

Laugh.

Tap.

Laugh.

"Mom." Chris stood. "What are you doing?"

She was about to give them a firm ass-chewing, the kind she'd give them when they were young and driving her up the wall with their antics as Hugh watched television in the living room, oblivious. But something caught her eye.

It was back.

The little gnome was back.

And it was tapping on her window.

Tap.

Laugh.

Tap.

Laugh.

"What the hell is that?!" Irene barely mustered the courage to point at it. Her feet were frozen to the kitchen tile, her limbs numb as if ants were crawling along them.

The gnome stared at her with fascinated green eyes and a long white beard that trailed to its midsection. Its body was painted blue beneath a layer of mud and broken in random places as if held together by some ungodly miracle. Its mouth was carved open in a laugh, revealing a set of broken teeth, many of them missing. A single finger tapped on the glass, as if it was a drinking bird, set to forever move back and forth in the same motion.

Hugh.

Her sons approached her, following her gaze.

"I said," she whispered shakily, "what the hell is that?"

It was silent for a long moment, then Benny lowered Irene's arm, never moving his gaze from the gnome.

"Mom, let's just back away slowly and go to your room."

"B-but the gnome! What if it gets inside?" Irene still couldn't take her eyes from it. It was so much like Hugh, she could nearly smell his earthy, decaying scent through the glass.

How was this possible?

Chris squeezed her other hand. "I'll lock the doors, okay? Just go with Benny, please."

"The gnome—it's Hugh. It's Hugh!"

The shrubs began to swallow the gnome, pulling it inside like a brambled mouth. Her legs nearly gave out from under her.

"Hurry, get it before it escapes! Quick!"

It took both Benny and Chris to carry her out of the kitchen and into her room. And all the while, she could hear it in the walls. He was coming for her.

Tap.

Laugh.

Tap.

"Is it still out there?"

Benny chewed on his lip the way he always did when he was in trouble or lying. Irene narrowed her eyes at him, waiting for the fib that was sure to come.

She lay in her bed as Benny knelt beside her. It had been a long night and Irene could barely keep her eyes open. Sleep was threatening to take her and she would welcome it if it weren't for the laughing in the distance and the tapping from the kitchen window.

"It's gone. Chris got rid of it, remember?"

"He's lying. I can still hear it out there."

Benny ignored her. "Chris went to work, so I'm going home now to get everything ready for you."

"I'm not going anywhere."

"Yes, you are. This is the fifth time this month—" He stood, shaking his head. "Never mind. Look, Mom, I love you, but I have to go. I'll be back tomorrow morning. Isaac will be stopping by later tonight. If you need anything, give me a call. Promise?"

She crossed her arms. "It'll take more than that gnome to kick me out of this house."

Benny let out a deep breath. "This would be so much easier if you just listened."

"No you listen," she snapped. "Your father is dead and somehow, even six feet under, he keeps bothering me. He's everywhere!"

Hugh's laughter filled the room and in a fit of rage, Irene threw a book from her bedside table at the wall. "Get out!"

"What is wrong with you?!" Benny retrieved the book, placing it on the windowsill. "You don't have to let Dad's death ruin you."

She could feel the anger building inside her as the room echoed with laughter, haughty and boisterous, as if he had gotten the upper hand. "I said get out!"

"We just want what's best for you!"

"I said, I'm not leaving." She emphasized the last words, then focused on the walls, the windows, wherever that godforsaken laughter was coming from. "Just die, Hugh! Die and leave me the hell alone!"

Benny flinched and moved slowly to the bedroom door. He turned the handle, but hesitated at the threshold. "Dad is gone. You need to move on."

She kept muttering insults at Hugh, at the gnome she was sure he was hiding inside of, at the rain that kept pouring outside, at everything and anyone that kept her from finding a modicum of peace.

Irene was bitter. She could feel it on her skin, she could taste it in her mouth. Hell, she could even see it in the blinding red that consumed her vision now.

Bitter.

She turned to her son, fresh curses on her tongue, but he was gone.

From the other side of the house, she heard the door lock.

Irene's kitchen was silent and dark even with the faint glow of the oven lamp. She could hear her heart beating in her ears, and somehow that was even worse than the laughter and tapping from earlier, which had since quieted.

It was nearly time, wasn't it?

She stared at the now-cold coffee in front of her untouched on the table. She wondered why she even bothered making a new cup at all. Occasionally, she would hear the house groan as it settled further into the foundation, and when she would look out the window, there was nothing but shrubs covering every inch. Gnomes tangled in their sharp, spindly embrace.

Dread pricked at the nape of her neck, reminding her that she was alone and somewhere, waiting for her, was Hugh.

The cuckoo clock chimed midnight, nearly giving her a second heart attack.

She swallowed, righting her shoulders.

There was a knock at the door.

Her eyes widened, her mouth went slack.

Another knock.

She couldn't find the will to speak.

Tap.

Laugh.

Tap.

Laugh.

She squeezed her eyes shut, hoping against hope that it would all stop. That she could finally live free and far away from Hugh and his endless taunts and gnomes and laughs. To live the life she wanted at the ripe old age of eighty-two.

"Happy anniversary."

She opened her eyes to find Hugh seated across from her in his blue suit. The only one that fit him at the funeral. His long, white beard was tangled like the shrubs and his green eyes, so much like the gnome's, stared down at her.

Irene slowly pushed the coffee cup toward him.

"Will this kill me?"

"Not anymore," she whispered, her lips trembling.

He took a sip and placed the mug down in front of him.

"This isn't real, you know." He gestured around them as the

shrubs broke through the glass, the gnomes reaching inside.

"You're not here."

"You saw to that." He tapped the mug.

"You're dead."

"I am."

"And I'm not."

"Not yet."

"Am I supposed to be?"

"Do you want to be?"

"No."

"Then who's drinking the coffee?"

"Me?"

Hugh opened his mouth to speak, but it wasn't quite Hugh anymore. His mouth was curled into a smile, his eyes like chipped paint on concrete. His suit was plastered to him like a second skin. The shrubs reached through the shattered windows, the deathly fingers of their branches curling around shards of glass.

"Then who is drinking the coffee?" he asked again, but the voice that echoed from his body wasn't his.

It sounded different.

Younger.

"Mrs. Delano?"

THE CORPSE

I DIDN'T EXPECT TO WAKE UP NEXT TO A CORPSE.

I certainly didn't think I would be so silent as I stared into its sunken eyes, at its bloated body. Every inch of me froze at the sight of it, my voice gone into hiding, my eyes never wavering from the missing teeth and far off stare. I couldn't budge as I took in the way its bloodied hair fell over half of its face. I couldn't tell how young or old it was, only that it lay next to me in this basement like a discarded piece of garbage, lost and forgotten in time.

I knew now that when it came to fight or flight that I would freeze. And oddly enough, as I stared at the insects crawling around the body next to me, I was disappointed at my lack of action.

I wonder if this corpse was a "freeze," too.

I hear rummaging through the walls, and I think that it may be rats. And for some reason, the thought of rats pulls me from my thoughts and makes me move. I jump to my feet and take in my surroundings.

It's a dingy basement, because of course it is.

And I'm in here because I froze.

Just like I did with the corpse.

I didn't know how to fight, and I was never good at talking my way out of things.

It was too easy to grab me as I walked in the dark. The sounds of retro pop blared in my headphones because I needed a nostalgic pick-me-up.

I couldn't afford it. In this economy? Absolutely not.

Besides, work was only a twenty-minute walk.

There are sidewalks in this small town.

It was safe.

It wasn't my fault I had to work late.

There's the sound of something heavy toppling over and I turn toward it.

But it's not happening in the basement.

It's coming from beyond the door at the top of the stairs.

A single bulb with a pull chain lingers just above it, providing just enough light so I can see the corpse has a purple jacket and green sneakers. I wonder if they tried to run, too.

There's cursing, and a deep voice grows close.

I step back into the dark.

"How do I get out of here," I whisper to no one.

Though, I suppose the corpse can hear me.

I stare back down at it, and it makes my limbs quiver.

Would I look like it, too?

If the person on the other side of the door makes his way down to me?

Yes, his.

I remember that at least.

He asked me something as he lingered between Cam's Grocery and The Corner Laundromat. I was only a block away from home and was craving some ramen noodles and trash TV. I had a shitty day at work and needed something to comfort me.

Maybe that was my problem. I was too focused on the wrong things as I walked with my hands in my pockets and keys in my purse.

I know, I know.

I should have kept them in a wolverine-like grip between my knuckles, ready to strike at the first sign of danger. But again, I wasn't focused and my pockets were too small. And honestly, I was just ready to go home.

I couldn't hear what he was saying and kept walking—didn't even think twice. Have you ever had someone wave in your direction and you wave back like a dork, kind of excited about a new interaction, but then they stare at you confused. And then, as they get closer, you see their eyes shift behind your shoulder and realize they were waving at someone behind you?

It's that kind of humiliation that, the next time someone waves in your direction, makes you think no one is actually approaching you. It's like some natural instinct to prevent embarrassment, when really in cases like mine, it keeps you from running like a bat out of hell because surely, that man was not talking to me.

A scream pierces the thick air of the musty basement. It's coming from the other side of the door. There's something happening up there, and I am selfish because I want it to stay there. I don't want to know what will happen to me if the door opens.

Will I scream, too, like that?

The street was otherwise empty, the lampposts the city council neglected to fix flickering weakly in the dark. One gave up and succumbed to its fate, hanging useless with a broken bulb barely clinging to the stray wires. My ears were consuming "Sweet Dreams" by the Eurythmics. You know that one part of the bridge where Annie Lennox keeps insisting you should hold your head up, keep your head up? It's the part where I would usually start dancing side to side before the instrumental payoff. It's hard to explain—you'd just have to listen to it.

I didn't expect him to grab me.

And I didn't think that he would pull me so quickly between the grocery store where I bought my apples and the laundromat that never spit out the right change. I screamed, I'm sure of it. But I don't know if anyone heard me, or if anyone cared.

You see, where I live, we're so busy. Everyone works and no one plays. We're all bone tired after a long shift and eat quick meals or order delivery because we don't have the brain power to think about cooking. My scream could have been someone's TV on the other side of the wall, that damn neighbor you've complained about to management a hundred times who for some reason never gets in trouble.

My scream could have been a joke, one made for a quick laugh on camera. A "you'd have to be there to get it" kind of video that isn't meant to scare anyone but through editing will make so much more sense.

You get it.

So, I screamed as Annie Lennox told me to hold my head up. My throat was raw by the time he muffled it with a dirty rag and pulled me into the dark.

Dammit, Annie, I should have listened.

But what I'm hearing on the other side of the door sends chills down my spine. I know, it's cliché to say, but really, it does. It's like that feeling you get when someone tells you to peek around a dark corner.

You tell yourself it's a surprise, something good. But then why do you get this unsettling feeling that what may lie around the corner is your worst nightmare come to life? In a split second, you wonder if you can really trust the person gesturing you there—if they've only pretended to be your friend for years just to lead you to this moment where they would feed you to whatever lies around the corner.

Okay, I'm getting off track.

There's banging now against the door. As if someone is kicking it, pushing themselves away from it. There's a lot of struggling going on, I can hear it, but fuck, I'm frozen. Why the hell do I keep freezing? Why couldn't I fight or flight, anything but sitting like a deer in headlights as if that would make the boogeyman go away.

Oh, she's no fun to chase. I'll just go find something else more exciting then.

Excitement.

That's why men like him do this to girls like me, right? I'm sure I read that somewhere in a magazine or saw it on TV when I flipped through the channels, wanting something to fill the silent space of my studio apartment. They are sociopaths, psychopaths, all the paths except the ones that lead home. Because I let my guard down and he saw me as a gift-wrapped opportunity for the taking. No one wants to go outside at night anymore, we're all so tired, we just want to lie at home and rot. Even if that means ignoring the screams in the street.

I move back and accidentally step on the corpse's hand. I hear the sickening crunch of its fingers beneath my sneakers. A bug skitters out from under it and back into the dark.

"Sorry," I whisper shakily, removing my foot.

The corpse doesn't move; it just lies there. The way it will lie there for the rest of its existence until it is swallowed up into the earth by the bugs or rats in the walls. But if I can make it out, maybe it can go back home, too.

Home.

My heart pounds like concert drums in my ears. I turn quietly, searching for an escape route, as if my movement would somehow get the attention of whoever's screaming and fighting upstairs. There's no longer banging against the door, but I can still hear a struggle not too far away.

I hope whoever she is makes it.

I hope she gets away...

And I hope I do, too.

There's a boarded-up window to my left, bits of sunlight creeping in through the cracks. I rush to it and somehow my adrenaline comes to life again. I try to pull the planks that are fastened there by bolts that have rusted over time. I can see faint scratches in the plywood, bits of blood, chipped nails. I'm beginning to think the corpse was not the first to be here. To die here.

How long was the man watching me?

Did he know my schedule, my normal day-to-day routine?

Did he follow me home from work on other days, when I was in a better mood?

Did he know which apartment I lived in?

Did he know that I was thinking about getting a dog, like my mom told me to?

Or the pepper spray I would see in the convenience store next to the keychain display?

Is it my fault that I didn't prepare for something like this to happen to me?

I bet that's what you're thinking.

If only I had thought about these things before and acted on them, then I wouldn't be standing in the basement of some man's house trying to escape whatever fate awaits the girl upstairs, or that of the corpse on the dirty floor.

Because instead of daydreaming about what my life could look like, I should have taken notes of the nightmares that could have come true.

That's more realistic, right?

Girls like me can't afford to dream—not when we may be snatched up on the walk home in the middle of the night, screaming our lungs out for a few precious milliseconds before the world goes dark.

But I don't think you understand.

We are tired, so bone-tired.

We are like the corpse that lies at the bottom of the basement stairs, its hands splayed out as if it were reaching for help but couldn't muster the energy to do much else. Even if it meant life or death.

And I did what I could, okay?

I listened to the podcasts about women who faced the terrors of the real world, I read the articles, I watched the shows. Surely some part of me checked a box there.

You don't think so?

Well, I did.

And secretly you do too.

Because we tell ourselves that listening to their stories is enough armor to shield us from what might happen. Our voices would be loud enough to wake the sun at night. Our fight would be worthy of a heavyweight championship. Our survival skills would carry us to safety no matter the situation. All because we listened to other stories, we collected notes and did the research.

But nothing truly beats first-hand experience.

I claw at the planks, tearing at them with whatever strength I can rally as I hear the terrifying screams. It's right outside the door. It's so close it could touch me, so close I feel it inside my bones. It's wrapping me in its embrace, promising that I'm next.

I'm losing nails, my fingers are getting splintered, there's a crack in the wood as I pull with all my might.

There's a thud. A single, nausea-inducing thud at the door.

It's quieter now. I hear heavy, heavy breathing on the other side of the door. The corpse lingers at the bottom of the steps, its purple jacket torn, its hair damp from all the blood. It's missing fingernails and is wearing a single silver moon ring like something you'd find at a thrift store.

I'm tugging at the plank, because my life depends on it. Silence be damned—time is running out. The wood finally groans and cracks and I rip it from the bolt.

The man must have heard me because he's grunting against something and cursing in hurried breaths like a wild, feral animal as he tries to open the door.

The plank is in my hands and, with what little strength I have, I hit the window with it. Glass shatters across the floor, tiny sparkles catching the dim light of the bulb with the pull chain.

I shove myself up, cutting my body on the sharp edges, not caring about the slashes I'm getting. But then I see it.

Metal bars on the outside.

Meant to keep me inside.

I scream in terror and frustration.

The man has opened the door.

He doesn't even look my way.

He throws a body inside.

And closes the door.

It topples down the stairs.

And falls on top of my purple jacket.

Because it's me, isn't it?

I'm the corpse on the basement floor.

PART III

MY SLEEP DEMON

It's appeared again. My sleep demon in the corner of the room.

He taunts me, beckons me in the middle of the night as I lie in my bed frozen in terror.

I am incapable of speaking, of moving, of begging for help or mercy, though I am not sure which would get me out of here faster.

Try as I might, I can't pull my gaze from it, forced to witness its presence as it lingers. My breathing is shallow and quiet, so unlike the screams I long to release.

My sleep demon stays in its corner during these visits; so close and yet it can see how I struggle, how I stare back at it with glossy eyes and twitching fingers.

He has taken many forms, but tonight's is simply the shadow creeping along the wall—tall and eerily thin, reaching the top of my ceiling like a neglected tree. Its face is obscured by the darkness that surrounds it, except for his mouth. That smile.

My sleep demon whispers my name like an incantation.

My sleep demon knows I have heard it—it can always read my thoughts. It smiles too wide and blood trickles from where its mouth should be and onto my carpet.

Tears roll down my cheeks.

It covers the nightlight I switched on for good measure, hoping it would prevent these visits.

It reaches its cloaked, bony fingers out and grazes my foot, tucked underneath the blanket. This is something it wasn't able to do before...touch me.

I am begging my body to cooperate, to move. I don't want to know what happens if I succumb to it. I don't want to be here, in this room, in this bed, alone with it.

Time has only strengthened its tether to me; it knows my darkest secrets, my deepest fears. It taunts my pain and mocks my struggles.

It is me.

At my highest, it reminds me of its presence.

I will never leave you. Ever.

At my lowest, it attempts to lure me to it.

I can do it for you, you know.

This time, it simply laughs.

Why must it always laugh?

I am useless, staring at the horror unfolding in front of me. Dread fills the pit of my stomach. My heart has given up—I can no longer hear it beating in my ears.

The smell of iron overwhelms my nostrils.

I squeeze my eyes shut.

This is what it wants.

This is how it wants me to...

MY EYES

"My eyes!" I screamed. "Look in my eyes, these aren't mine!"

The doctor took his time to meet my gaze, resigned. Almost as if I were telling him again that the weather was going to be poor outside.

His eyes crinkled at the corners, his long wiry beard hanging low past his chest. His hair was messy, and he tilted his head slightly.

"Hmm." He smiled. "I don't see anything wrong."

"There is something wrong, I'm telling you!" I panicked, trying to get up from the bed, but something was holding me down.

The doctor ignored me, turning instead to a nurse with caked-on makeup that looked sweated through, who was taking notes at his side.

"Do you see something wrong?" he asked her.

She raised a brow, rather uninterested. "It's your finest work, Doctor."

She continued to take notes.

Everything was hazy. I was no longer in a doctor's office of bright whites and light gray cabinetry. No longer did the sun filter in through the window behind me.

This place was dark and rotted, with only a single illuminated surgical light above me, rocking back and forth like a pendulum. Insects crawled in and around the padded velvet walls. They tried to crawl to me, too, and I shooed them away in terror.

"It's all in your head, dear." The doctor's smile did not reach his eyes, and he patted my hand as if to comfort me.

"Let me see a mirror. Let me see my eyes!"

I could hear the buzzing of the insects, a motor in the distance, groans for help outside the walls. They were knocking, as if begging me to let them in.

"They're coming for me!" I yelled.

"I'm sure they are," he replied. He turned to the nurse. "Please see to it that the patient is sedated. Rest is her only remedy."

"A mirror!" I pleaded.

The doctor gave me a nod and left the room, disappearing into the darkness beyond. The nurse set about tinkering with the objects on the bedside table.

"Please," I begged, grabbing her arm. It felt like touching dirt. "Let me see my eyes."

"Patience is a virtue," she chided, brushing off my hand, "but since you were such a good patient..."

I could see the insects climbing on her scrubs, following her left hand into her pocket. She retrieved a small compact mirror, opening it.

"There's nothing to worry about," she said. "Dr. Frank is quite talented. It's normal for patients to have this reaction at first."

She shook off the bugs that crawled across the glass, lifting the mirror so I could see better.

I screamed in horror.

My eyes were glossy and decaying. A yellowish film, thick and semi-translucent, covered irises that were once blue. I whipped my head to the side and the mirror in her hands clattered to the ground, scaring away the bugs there. The groans were louder now, begging, pleading as I was. I thrashed against my bindings on the bed, screaming out for help.

"See?" The nurse smiled calmly and lifted a large needle. "Good as new."

The surgical light flickered.

"See, good as new," the doctor said warmly.

I blinked, and everything around me was as it was before. The bright white room, the gray cabinets, the cheery doctor who reminded me of Santa Claus. Behind him was the nurse, except she now looked polished and inviting.

"Just as I said, there's nothing to worry about." The doctor faced the nurse. "It's normal for patients to have this reaction at first. Patience is a virtue." He made a point of waving his finger around to emphasize his words.

The nurse nodded and took notes on a clipboard.

"Please," I begged, my voice barely audible. I felt so weak. "Let me see my eyes."

The doctor continued to speak to the nurse, but I could barely make out their words.

"A mirror!" I tried to scream, but my voice was hollow.

"...and please see to it that the patient is sedated. Rest is her only remedy."

"They're coming for me!" I yelled, remembering now the groans through the wall.

The doctor turned to me. Somehow, my voice had finally reached his ears.

"It's all in your head, dear." The doctor's smile reached his eyes, and he patted my hand to comfort me.

"It's your finest work, Doctor." The nurse beamed, a look of pride on her face.

"There is something wrong, I'm telling you!" I choked out.

"Hmm." He smiled, leaning in to inspect my eyes with his ophthalmoscope. "I don't see anything wrong."

"My eyes!" I tried once more to scream, but it came out as a whimper. "Look in my eyes, these aren't mine!"

"Now, now." The doctor stood up straighter. "That would just be madness, wouldn't it?"

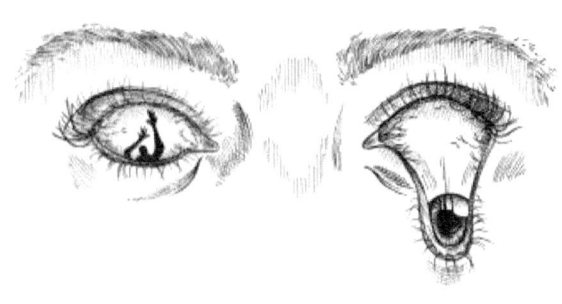

LILIANA

She was the midnight to my summer sun,
The last strained breath upon my tongue,
A bitter memory of painful regret,
The nightmare to my vintage dreams,
Liliana, my dear,
Will you come back to me?

Amado read the words again.

It had to be perfect this time.

He folded the edges of the page carefully and sealed the envelope. He blew on the wax, cooling it into submission. Time was of the essence.

He nearly flew from the doors of his hacienda, jumping on his mare and giving her a swift kick with his riding boots. The harsh wind whipped at his coattails, his heart thundering in his chest, aching for the touch of his sweet Liliana.

She was all he could see when he closed his eyes, the only light in the bitter, dreary skies that plagued his days and nights since they'd met. His horse pounded against the muddy path, racing faster than the desert rain could catch them. It was half a day's ride to her, and there he hoped she would be, because all he had to say was more than this letter could convey.

He needed her to take him more than he needed air.

"She is new here, a distant relative who inherited Fidencio's land out east."

"A Doña, then," Amado remarked, glancing to where his friend gestured. The woman wore a crimson gown with black lace details that lined the hem and bodice of her dress. It was quite scandalous considering most women at this party were dressed in modest frocks, bland in color and laced up to their necklines. This woman wanted to stand out—she wanted to be remembered. And remembered she would be.

Her eyes were a curious mix of browns and greens, a hazel rich as the earth. Her lips, like the Spanish roses that grew in his garden, made him nearly forget to breathe. She twirled in the arms of a local lawyer, Tomás, and no doubt this poor fool had fallen in love as the music crescendoed and the woman held his eyes with hers like a promise.

Amado felt as if he was intruding on something intimate. He would have turned away, busied himself in some other conversation, but he couldn't. He would have given his soul to the woman without question, even begged her to take more of him. It was the strangest feeling.

"What is her name?" Amado breathed, watching as the dance ended and the man kissed the woman's hand.

"I'm not certain," his friend said, "but there's not much known about her. My wife says she likes to keep to herself."

Amado met his friend's eyes. "With all of Fidencio's land, I can imagine she must have her hands tied."

"I suppose so. Though, I am certain she will be married before the end of the season. Look at how these men lust after her." He pointed to an elder gentleman sitting in the corner and laughed. "Even our mayor is smitten. I wonder what his wife will say."

Amado tried to focus. He might have even mustered a weak laugh, but something pulled him back to the woman. She was alone in the middle of the crowded room, Tomás nowhere to be seen.

When she faced him, all hope was lost.

Her hazel eyes—how mystifying they were—met his gaze. Her long, dark hair was pinned back effortlessly from her face and trailed down her back in soft curls. The corners of her mouth lifted into a gentle smile and he wondered how it would feel to press his lips to hers.

This woman was beckoning him, he was certain. She had cast aside Tomás and now Amado was the lucky one, chosen from a room full of other wealthy suitors. He felt his legs moving toward her, following her out of the governor's home and into the gardens outside as if lured by an invisible tether.

The way he would follow her into fire if she wished.

A rare cool breeze graced the gardens, carrying the flitting whispers of couples engaged in illicit dalliances to his ears. They hid behind the trees and within the garden maze, flirting with risk and pleasure. He was certain the governor was among them somewhere.

Amado tried to ignore them all as he followed the woman toward the cast stone statues on the far end, carved ornately by some artist he couldn't recall the name of. She stood facing them, running her fingers along the stone.

A delicious thrill ran through him. The candlelight of the home did not do her justice—so close, she was perfection defined in the flesh.

"I do so love admiring what is beautiful," she said, peeking at him from beneath her lashes, her fingers following the bends and grooves of the statue before her.

"Yes," he breathed, then cleared his throat. "As do I."

She stopped and turned slowly to him.

"Do you think me beautiful, Amado?"

"Yes."

He wanted so very badly to touch her, to feel her skin against his. To feel the beating of her heart against his chest.

She walked to him slowly, her eyes never wavering from his. The wind carried the scent of roses to him. It was intoxicating and maddening. He would sooner gouge his eyes out than disappoint her, and only far off in his mind did he ponder how strange a declaration that was.

"W-what is your name, my darling?" he managed.

The woman wrapped her hands around his shoulders and pulled him close to her. His lips trembled in anticipation of what was sure to come.

Did she feel it, too?

He vaguely noticed the absence of her heartbeat as their bodies pressed together as one. Though he did not care to give it a second thought—an angel was in his arms demanding his undivided attention.

She lifted her lips to his ear, and whispered.

"Liliana."

Liliana.

Amado woke from his sleep, his sheets soaked through with sweat, his heart threatening to leave his body. He took in his room. It was dark and warm and the night sky was shrouded in dark gray clouds, pregnant with a rare rain. Thunder rolled in the distance.

He wasn't sure how he'd gotten home, only that the name Liliana was a mantra grounding his sanity. Amado turned to the empty side of his bed, at first convinced that she had accompanied him home. But when his fingers brushed the sheets, they were cold, much like his soul without her.

Troubled, he took off his night shirt and went to the window, as if the world outside would find her for him and transport her there. The scent of roses flooded his senses, and just beyond the gates of his home, he swore he saw those beautiful hazel eyes staring back at him.

"Liliana, my dear," he whispered, "come save my wretched soul."

It was a week of troubled sleep and dreams of her in his arms before he saw Liliana again. She walked along the town streets in a sapphire-blue dress, her pretty face shielded from the rain beneath a dark umbrella. Amado nearly forgot to breathe. Seeing her in the flesh was more than he could bear. She was even more radiant than his fickle memories could fathom. His dreams of her so sorely lacked the potency of her true beauty.

Her carriage waited for her outside of the apothecary's shop, the coachman holding a second umbrella and the carriage door for his Doña. She took the first step inside just as Amado reached her. The rain soaked his suit and hair.

"Liliana," he called desperately.

She turned, raising a brow.

"Liliana, I need to speak with you—"

Amado didn't finish his words. A man peeked out from inside the carriage—Tomás.

Liliana placed her hand in Tomás' and he helped her to her seat.

"Liliana," Tomás asked, "do you know this man?"

She looked at Amado with curious eyes, tilting her head in confusion. "I have never seen him before in my life."

Devastation came swift.

"Liliana," Amado begged, refusing to let the coachman close the carriage door. "Please. We met at the governor's house, we were in gardens, we—"

"How dare you speak so salaciously of the Doña," Tomás said. "She was with me that night."

"No! It's not true—tell him, Liliana! Tell him." Amado couldn't understand why this upset him so. After only a week he could scarcely imagine his life without her, and seeing her with this man would drive him to insanity.

Without a doubt, he had clung to their brief moment in the garden—he was certain she wanted him as much as he longed for her. The way she held him, so close...

"Stop now and carry on with your day, sir, or I shall be forced to speak to the sheriff of this encounter!" Tomás declared.

Liliana's eyes watered, filling with fear as she stared at Amado.

How could she ever fear him!

"Please leave," she cried. "I do not want anything to do with you."

Tomás held her hand. "Not to worry, my dear. He will be out of our sight soon."

The coachman shoved Amado aside and closed the door, but Amado was not done yet. He did not care if he made a spectacle in the street.

He leapt to the side of the carriage. "Tell him, Liliana! Tell him of the gardens!"

Tomás pushed Amado off of the carriage door and the coachman whipped the horses into a trot. Amado fell into a puddle on the street, more desperate than ever for Liliana.

The woman of his dreams.

There she was again.

Liliana stood at the foot of his bed.

She wore the same crimson dress from the governor's house and stared down at Amado with a pleasant smile.

"Liliana," he whispered, "is that you?"

"Shhh," she hushed him, moving to his side of the bed.

"Y-you said you wanted nothing to do with me." Amado did not realize how wretched he felt in her presence.

She held a hand to him, and he grasped it like a dying man reaching for water. He kissed it tenderly.

"You must not say a word," she breathed, pulling her hand back slowly.

The loss of her touch nearly brought him to tears.

Liliana bent down to him, and her eyes—how they tied him to the earth. How enchanting they were. Amado felt the slow rise and fall of his chest despite his rapid heartbeat, faster than he ever thought humanly possible. Her lips were mere inches from his and waited for his answer.

You must not say a word.

He could hear her voice inside his head. He could feel her in his flesh. She was everywhere and still he wanted more. He couldn't live if he didn't have more.

"I swear it."

"You are mine, Amado," she whispered, her voice a siren's call in an ocean of bewitched sailors. The things he would do to stay in her favor.

"I am yours, Liliana. Forever."

Liliana,

My heart aches for you.
I close my eyes and dream of you.
There you visit me.
And there we spend eternity.
Forever yours, as promised,

Amado

He woke again to an empty bed and cold sheets. He shivered as the rain pelted his window, goosebumps prickling his skin uncomfortably. It was a sickness, he was sure of it, this obsession with Liliana—his unsatisfied and wholly desperate desire for her.

Food did not taste as it once did.

Water from the well did not quench his thirst.

And idle conversation amongst the gentlemen did not captivate his interests.

So badly, he wished to see Liliana again.

But his promise to her kept him hollow, cast in the darkness of his daymares every second he did not feel her touch.

And so he wrote his frustrations away and sent letters with his courier, hoping against hope that she would write him back and save him from his misery.

A misery that plagued his days and disappeared in the nights she would come to him.

The second time Amado laid eyes on Liliana outside of his lonely room was at another party at the home of a prominent businessman. He attended only in hopes that Liliana would be there. Perhaps he would be able to speak to her privately and beg for a moment in her presence.

His friends were gathered, discussing the state of the country, the rain that had come from nowhere and showed no sign of stopping, and a war that had extinguished everything but the fire in the eyes of the working class. Amado could barely hear them, their voices far gone as his eyes searched the space for those of browns and greens and earth. His fingers trembled against the glass in his hand, the lack of sleep taking its toll on him at last.

He considered leaving for the briefest of moments, but then he finally saw her. He let out a single, relieved breath. All his worries had vanished. He was no longer deprived of sleep, his vigor was restored, his hands no longer shook. He felt himself standing taller amongst the gentlemen.

She walked inside in a burgundy dress fitted tight against her waist. Her neckline was draped just over her shoulders, revealing her collarbone and the jewels affixed atop them. Every head in the room turned to look at her, and she turned to the entrance and smiled at someone just out of sight.

She reached her hand across the threshold and someone took it gingerly.

No.

Tomás followed her into the room, kissing her hand just as Amado once had. She smiled up at him and Tomás placed her hand in the crook of his elbow. They walked elegantly into the room as the musicians played a familiar tune, breaking the spell as the partygoers returned to their gossip.

Amado could not believe what he was seeing. His hands shook again and he fled the room, not wishing to witness her with that miserable excuse of gentleman. He ran out to the back patio, where a soft drizzle greeted him, and fell against the wall, trying to stay upright as his heart sank into a pit of despair.

The rain pooled at the ends of his tendrils and fell like his tears onto the terracotta floors. He was a wretched tangle of bitterness and desperation. He could not fathom why she would seek another when he had done everything she had asked of him in the midnights leading up to this night.

"Do you often cry in the rain?"

Amado turned to the voice. It was not his Liliana, but another woman he would have once thought beautiful. She wore a simple, pale pink dress with white lace trim along the edges. Her hair was braided neatly and fastened with pins. She had a faint, rosy tint to her cheeks that was more charming than alluring.

Amado wiped his face with the back of his suit sleeve.

"No, not often."

She stayed under the cover of the archway as she spoke. "She must be beautiful to evoke such wretchedness in you."

"It doesn't matter."

"Can I help?"

Amado turned to the windows facing the inside of the room. They glowed with candlelight and inside, Liliana rested her head against Tomás' arm. A sickening jealousy filled him.

"I'm not certain anyone can." He set about to leave, walking toward the arched doorway where the woman stood just out of the rain. He was glad he'd told his footman to stay behind and wait for him.

"Heartbreak makes us do mad things," the woman said, reaching for his hand as he made to pass her. Her touch was warm, unlike the cool rain that sprinkled around them. "And I am heartbroken, too."

Amado stared down at the woman, who met his gaze with equal frankness. "I am not in need of love," he said, turning his head toward where Liliana stood with Tomás. "I simply want to rid myself of it."

The woman reached her hand up to his cheek and turned his head to meet her gaze. "As do I."

Her dark brown eyes were like those of a doe—so sweet. "I'm Amado," he said.

"Mariana," she whispered.

They left the party together before Amado could stop himself.

Trying to rid himself of thoughts of Liliana in the arms of Tomás.

That evening, as Mariana left his home, Amado stared once more out the window. He watched as the carriage passed the gates and turned left toward the town where surely someone awaited her. The carriage crested the hill and was soon out of sight.

The rain fell heavy against the glass, a thick fog clinging to it like a desperate lover. When he raised a hand to it, it felt like ice against his flesh. How cold and desolate his soul had become.

Amado had whispered many things to the woman as they shared their misery in the tangled sheets. He'd nearly forgotten how warm skin felt against his fingertips, how heady a kiss could be when lips shared the same purpose.

And still, it was Liliana's name he called out.

Even in ecstasy, she did not give him a moment of peace.

He could see her face in place of Mariana's, could feel her rose-colored lips on his. Her hazel eyes as they promised him the world and more.

His heart ached for her. He wanted her.

He needed her.

"Oh, Liliana, what have I done?"

She visited him that night as he woke from a fitful sleep. A nightmare of darkness and despair clutched him tight and he gasped awake at the witching hour. Lightning cracked and Liliana crawled to him from the edge of his bed.

"You have betrayed me, my dear," she whispered to him, her words like poison.

Amado nearly forgot to breathe. Where he should have felt fear, there was only euphoria. She had returned to him. She wanted him, too.

Liliana was so close that they shared the same air. The scent of roses filled the space, a welcoming, intoxicating scent that hazed his senses.

"I will not visit you again."

The words brought him back to her. Panic rippled through him, ripping him apart from the inside.

"No, my love," Amado begged, "I saw you with Tomas. I thought you did not want me."

Liliana's lips brushed Amado's as she spoke. "This is unforgivable, Amado."

She wore the crimson dress he so longed to remove from her. His hands were tangled in her hair in overwhelming desperation. A midnight offering promising daylight regret. He could not live without her, would not live without her.

"I will never do it again, I promise," he declared, "I will do anything."

She appeared now as a ghost on his bed, moving between something that felt real and something that vanished at his touch. She
was slipping through his fingers.

"I can never look at her again without thinking of what you did."

"I will never see her again. I will never be where she is. Pl—"

He didn't finish his words.

Liliana was gone.

Amado did not sleep for three days and three nights. He begged for Liliana to return to his bed, writing her letters nearly every hour. His courier would return only to be given another batch of letters to take to the Doña. His staff worked around the clock, as Amado would usher them to his room to speak of nothing but Liliana and the need for more ink and parchment.

His letters grew in desperation and intensity, inconsolable scribbling on the page that made little sense and was utterly illegible to his staff, who secretly opened them to see what plagued their Don Amado. He refused to eat, and not even his favorite dishes could coax him from his chamber. He was not particularly skilled as an artist, but he would sketch the Doña in many of his letters to her as tokens of his commitment.

If the staff had not convinced Amado that the Doña was away visiting family, they were certain he would have walked barefoot in the desert rain to her.

As he paced on the third night, Amado thought once more of Liliana's parting words.

"I can never look at her again without thinking of what you did."

Having reviewed his ledgers, he knew it was quite possible to give up his family hacienda and take Liliana far from this place, away from where Mariana would certainly be.

But what if that was not enough?

Liliana deserved to be safe in the knowledge that she would never cross paths with that woman. He needed to prove to her that he was willing to do anything for her.

Anything for Liliana.

Amado watched from a distance, hidden by night and rain, as Mariana brushed her hair in the second story of her family's home in town. She sat at her vanity next to a single lit candle, the soft wind pushing the curtains of her room gently to and fro.

There she was.

And there she wasn't.

He climbed the adobe wall surrounding her home with ease,

nothing on his mind but his dear Liliana.

The rest of the home was shrouded in darkness and Amado made his way inside and up the stairs, quietly tiptoeing his way to Mariana.

It wasn't enough to kill for her.

Liliana still did not show that night.

Nor the night after.

Nor the night after that.

Amado couldn't sleep, his body's withered distress betraying his expected vitality.

He wrote to her once more, but did not beckon the courier.

He would wait in her home even if it took weeks for her to return.

Amado arrived at Liliana's hacienda as thunder roared in the distance. The rain had caught up with him, drenching his coat.

Her home was immaculate, the thick walls covered in stucco so light that it was nearly consumed by the shadow of overcast skies, and appeared a haunting, astonishing gray. The building was wider than it was tall, stretching across the expansive acre of land it rested on. So grand was the detail and tilework of the roof and steps that led to her front double doors that Amado nearly tripped admiring the workmanship. The archway appeared to have been crafted by something holy or unholy, delicate artwork adorning the wood finishings.

He could never imagine leaving such a place.

A woman opened the door before he had a chance to knock.

"Yes?" she said curtly. "Can I help you?"

She was an older woman, her face etched with lines of hardship and stress. Her hands were callused and her eyes tired. It was clear she was a maid or cook in the house. Amado removed his hat respectfully.

"May I see the Doña Liliana?" he asked, fumbling with it

between his fingers.

She eyed him warily. No doubt Amado looked miserable, if not despondent. "And who are you?"

"I am Don Amado. I have sent letters to your Doña," he began.

"Yes, we have received them, Señor."

"Has she returned from her visit with family? My staff did not say when she would be back." He nearly dropped his hat, so nervous was he to see her. How badly he wanted to feast his eyes upon her. He tried to peek inside over the woman's head to see if he could catch a glimpse of Liliana.

The woman's eyes softened. "She will not be back for a while. But I will tell her as soon as she comes that you have paid her a visit."

Amado's heart sank. "Can I stay and wait for her?"

She flashed him a strange look. "My Doña would be most displeased. She may not wish to speak with you if you were to intrude on her home." She said the words carefully, slowly, as if she were speaking to a child who did not know right from wrong.

Amado thought to press the matter, but relented, not wishing to further harm Liliana. "I understand. But can you see that she gets this?" He handed her the letter from his coat pocket. It was damp, but mercifully it was not torn or distressed.

She took it. "Of course."

For good measure, Amado took one last look behind the woman, but the home seemed rather empty. His only solace in this matter was knowing that Liliana had not tossed his letters in a fire, but had simply not seen them yet.

He turned to leave, but the woman called out to him. "Leave, far from this place, mijo. Stay away until you can dream of sunlight again."

Amado was not sure what to make of her words, but nodded.

As he climbed onto his mare in the rain, he took one last, longing look at the home of Liliana. Oh, how it loomed before him like a grave over a corpse. It should have frightened him, but somehow, it felt right.

He would not listen to the woman.

Because he knew, somewhere deep inside he knew, he would return.

If only to see Liliana's beautiful face again.

"Doña, there is a letter for you."

Liliana did not turn to her maid, but instead gestured to the basket of letters beside her. She sat in her chaise lounge facing the window, reading a book that seemed to captivate her. Her hair was braided neatly in a single strand that reached below her breasts. Her long velvet dress pooled along the carpeted floor like blood on sheepskin. Her face was so immaculate in the candlelight that she had no need for the chiqueadores that had gained popularity among the noblewomen after the latest bout of smallpox had raged through the town last summer.

She never seemed to need much, save for...

The maid gently placed the letter on top of the pile and turned for the door when Liliana spoke. That familiar, unwelcome chill snaked up her spine.

"Madness will have more followers and hangers-on than sound sense..." the Doña said, eyes fixed on her book. "What do you think of that?"

The maid furrowed her brow, curious. "Is this from your book?"

"Yes." Liliana flipped the page, still not looking up from it. "But that is not the question."

The maid straightened. "I believe it to be true."

"As do I." She flipped the page again.

The maid swallowed, a lump forming in her throat. She did not like to be near the Doña for too long.

"I-is there anything else I can do for you?"

Liliana closed her book with a snap that startled the maid. She took a sharp breath, flinching.

Her Doña cocked her head and smiled gently. "I am quite hungry."

"Of course." The maid's lips trembled as she nodded. "I will see what I have left for you. Shall I—"

"No, I no longer long for the lawyer."

The maid stilled.

"But...what about the man who left me this?" Liliana plucked the letter from atop the pile and opened it. "He seems to be quite infatuated with me."

"Y-yes, he was." The maid bit her lip to keep from shaking.

"Did he say anything?"

"Only that he was desperate to see you, as they all are."

"Hmm." Liliana peered through the darkened window, her skirts rustling as she leaned forward. "It seems he is not too far."

"I am not sure he will return so late. He might have other engagements…"

Liliana stilled.

And the maid knew she had erred.

Her Doña turned slowly, folding the letter back into place. Her lips lifted into an enchanting smile. It would have felt welcoming if not for what lurked beneath her skin. She closed the distance between them, and the maid knew better than to run despite her mind's pleading screams.

As Liliana placed a cold hand on her cheek, a faint whimper escaped the maid's lips. "You are very special to me. I hope you stay special to me."

Her eyes were no longer a blend of browns and earthy greens, but black like her soul. Within them, the maid could see herself quiver with fear.

"I will," the maid breathed, her legs nearly buckling beneath her.

"I would like this man to join me for dinner."

"Yes, Doña."

Liliana unfolded the letter once more, re-reading the words etched on the parchment. She gave it a gentle kiss and looked at the maid, who could barely move.

"He will do quite nicely."

IT'S LONELY HERE

HERE YOU ARE AGAIN, READING THIS HORROR STORY, searching for some way to bring excitement to your life.

Maybe reading things like this soothes you to sleep, and you keep a copy of your favorite thriller on your bedside table with the sinister cover facing up.

It's what makes you cool.

It's what makes you feel different from everyone else.

But what about *us*?

What about the ones you're reading about?

Not the characters on the page, but the ones who sleep beneath your feet.

The ones time has forgotten and the dirt has swallowed.

The ones whose lives were taken too soon.

The ones whose lives were taken too violently.

We, too, were different from everyone else.

Can you then, with all your fascination, help us?

Can you solve the mysteries of our demise and restore our peace?

No?

You're just here for a good story?

Just here to pass the time?

I see.

Well, then.

Let us share ours…

We watch you while you sleep.

We lurk in the shadows in your room.

We hear how you breathe when the nightmares consume you.

The feeling you get when you're walking late at night when all is too quiet.

That's us, too.

And we make you think it's in your head.

You see, we see everything.

We hear everything.

We can feel everything.

It's how we pass the time.

Because it's lonely here where we are.

And we can't go back, can't change how we came to be here.

Nor can we stop what's coming for you, too.

So we'll wait

until the night

you become

one of us.

MY DREAMS COME TRUE

I ALWAYS KNEW THERE WAS SOMETHING STRANGE ABOUT SARA DIAZ. She would walk through the halls of Castle Ridge High with a slight smirk on her face, acting like she knew some secret that no one else did. As if she were part of some club that no one else was invited to that shared these secrets that no one else knew.

Okay, you get the point.

She was pretty, like the kind of girl you knew was smart and could tell you things you never knew you needed to hear, while also looking like she could turn heads if she really wanted to. She was never popular, though. From what I saw, she never had any friends and spent most of her time pretending to read a book.

Yeah, that's what I said, pretending to read a book.

I would see Sara in the school courtyard or in class, staring off into space or at air while holding a book in a grip so fierce I once thought the pages were going to slice her fingers right off. But it was more than just staring—sometimes she would mumble as if she were talking to someone. A few times she would even laugh out loud, or tears would stream down her face, or she would be arguing under her breath. I don't know. It was creepy.

And even if that wasn't the case, her long, dark hair covered most of the book and she never made the effort to pretend to flip the pages every now and then. As I said, she wasn't ever reading, she just used the book like a prop so everyone thought she was. When really, she was just looking at nothing.

So one time I decided to ask her about it. I didn't have a crush on her or anything, I just wanted to know what the hell she was staring at and if it had anything to do with the book.

I guess I should've mentioned, these books weren't anything special. It was a textbook one day, a library book the next, and once I even saw her holding a cookbook. I swear I'm not making it up.

Anyway, I go up to her and ask exactly that: "What're you staring at?"

She stared at me with the strangest expression, those big, brown eyes looking at me as if I were the one talking to air and playing play-pretend with books in broad daylight.

"It's my dream come true," she said.

Honest to fucking god, that's what she said.

I didn't even stay to ask her what the damn book was about, because what kind of answer was that?

It was like that all of high school. She was the weird kid no one wanted to be around because the rumors flowed whenever someone finally remembered she existed. She was a witch, a troll, on acid, maybe high, who knows. It was open season on Sara Diaz for a brief week or two before other things became more interesting. And the cycle would repeat.

When we graduated, I didn't hear anyone clap for her in the stands, just pin-drop silence as her name was called in the high school gym where we had our commencement ceremony. I didn't feel too bad until she began waving at nothing as she collected her diploma and no one waved back. So I decided to be a bit brave and wave in her direction, and while she gave me a puzzled look and moved on, I got my crush's number for being nice.

No, we never did get together.

Oh, me and Sara?

You have to listen, have some patience.

We all went our separate ways as people do when they graduate high school and leave for school or to work or just get high and blow the summer away. I did a bit of all three and went away to school in New York for a bit.

I had some fun out there—miss the nightlife—but sometimes I want to walk down a sidewalk and not see a monster rat coming down the street at me. I only stayed there for two years before I transferred back home to California State and did the commute from Union City. The drive wasn't too bad and I listened to my CD collection, back when CDs were the thing. I was into all kinds of stuff back then, but I think Alice in Chains was a favorite, for sure. I had to buy a second album after the CD kept skipping. I played it too much and still do sometimes.

Oh, Sara?

Yeah, I'm getting there.

So, I'm back from New York after a two-year stint, I got two more years to go before I can finish my degree, and I need a job. My buddy Kyle says he can hook me up at Greg's Burger Joint in town, so that's where I spent that summer. Flipping burgers, flirting with pretty girls, and being a menace to my parents. You know, normal stuff.

So one Tuesday, the slowest day of the week and the one where I usually closed by myself since no one ever bothered to show—which, by the way, all that money they spent on electricity just for one customer to order a burger in a six-hour window is wild. Money down the drain. My mom would've killed me if I left a light on for five minutes in my room.

Back on track now.

So Tuesday, I'm on the closing shift and in walks Sara Diaz ten minutes to closing. I wasn't completely surprised, we were close by our old high school. Honestly, I kind of figured she dropped off the face of the earth after graduation, but when I heard the jingle above the door and saw her standing there, I thought I saw a ghost. An honest to god ghost at Greg's Burger Joint.

I would've thought the weed I smoked in the back was finally rotting my brain like the anti-drug cops said at the pep rallies in school, but then she smirked like she always used to and walked toward me.

To be honest, it was almost like she floated, but I'll admit that one was probably the weed.

Then she dropped the smirk and gave me that same look she did the day I confronted her in the courtyard all those years ago.

"Have your dreams come true yet?" she asked.

Did she come here just to ask me that?

Did she not want a #1 with fries and a Coke?

I didn't know what to say so I rambled like I sometimes do when I'm nervous.

I told her, "No, I'm only just beginning. And besides, dreams are for sleep and I plan to spend the rest of my twenties rocking out and feeling alive."

I know it was a mouthful, but something about the way she was staring at me like she was looking through me made me feel like I had to fill in the blank spaces. The silence gave me the creeps.

She looked…I don't know, disappointed.

Was I supposed to have my whole life planned out at twenty?

So Sara leans in close, and I'm not going to lie, I thought she was going to plant one on me, but don't worry, I'm keeping this PG in case your kids try to go through the case files.

Oh, you don't actually bring them home?

Okay, well, that's a bummer.

Guess this isn't like the shows.

Anyway, she leans in close and says, "You need to let them in."

"Let what in? The door's open, but I'm about to close in five minutes."

"No," she said, "you need to let them in."

She left quickly after that as if all of a sudden she realized she reached her word quota of the year or something and had to hide back in her room before curfew. She didn't even have a car that I could tell—I saw her through the burger joint windows running down the sidewalk until she turned right at the corner store.

At the time, I thought that someone made her stop by, like a prank or something. She certainly ran like someone who ding-dong-ditched. But if I'm being honest—which of course I am here, sir— I didn't even think twice about it. It was definitely not the weirdest encounter I'd had with late night dwellers. So, I closed up my shift, locked the doors and went home. Left the conversation far behind me as I jammed to Hate to Feel. It's a classic now, but at the time it was peak grunge. Anyone can fight me about it.

Oh, yes, I'll get back on track.

I forgot about the whole thing.

That was until I fell asleep.

I had a dream that I was walking around my high school. It was empty, like it usually was in the summer, and dark, but not pitch black. I wasn't scared or anything, it's just that feeling you get when your dream body knows what it's doing, it's floating between space and time, in and out of different scenes, and your mind is just along for the ride. Or maybe it's that your mind is the ride and your dream body is going around trying to hold on for dear life. I'm not sure, I didn't major in philosophy.

So, I was walking through the halls, and they seemed to stretch for miles. I called out for anyone but my voice just carried all the way down. But it didn't echo—there didn't seem to be an end to this hall.

I walked by the classrooms and saw the one that belonged to my English teacher, Mr. Cordova, who passed away a year ago from some kind of cancer. May he rest in peace, he was a nice guy.

His Welcome to English 401 sign with his name attached to the bottom was taped to the door. The hall was feeling too lonely, and I knew I was getting nervous because the echo still hadn't come back and my stomach dropped to my ass.

I pushed the door open and walked inside. It looked just like I remembered, even with his cheesy posters, like one that read Raise Your Hand with a shooting star. But it was empty. Just like the hallway, the room was empty of anyone else. It was just me, walking around like it was some museum or shrine to Mr. Cordova. But I think what got me the most was how quiet it was.

I can't handle the quiet. It's why I talk so much. When things are quiet, I just remember things.

But I'm not there yet. Let me finish my thought before I forget.

Mr. Cordova was cool because he was an easy grader and would talk to us like we weren't little kids. And every Friday he would pull in the class TV and play a movie for us while we just hung out. Even kids from other classes would sneak into Mr. Cordova's because he welcomed everyone there.

"I'd rather have students in school than out there making trouble for themselves," he used to say.

And it was true.

Even Sara once popped in on Friday during fourth period, when I knew she had gym because I would see her and the other girls running around the track from Mr. Cordova's second floor window. I liked my seat next to the window because I liked to look outside and daydream, it helped me focus better if that makes any sense.

She wasn't bad at gym, she was actually a decent sprinter and if she worked on the form she could've been a good hurdler, but like I said, she didn't have any friends, so it was obvious she didn't enjoy it.

Yes, fourth period. Mr. Cordova.

She stopped in one day when we were watching Wishbone. It was a kid's thing, but because it was better than writing essays and everyone respected Mr. Cordova, we all paid attention and pretended to take notes like Sara pretended to read books.

Tessa was out sick that day, so the desk next to me was free and Sara sat there. No questions asked. Mr. Cordova didn't even drop his newspaper to see if she was one of his students. He was just that kind of guy.

The next week, Tessa was sick again. Apparently this time it was food poisoning and there again right next to me was Sara.

Then the same thing happened the next week.

Then the next.

And then we found out that Tessa had some nervous breakdown and her parents decided to move her to a different school. It was crazy because Tessa was always funny and loud and we could joke about things in class whenever we were together. But just like that, she was gone. I was a bit bummed—Tessa was a nice girl.

So there I am in my dream, walking around Mr. Cordova's classroom and feeling a sense of nostalgia because it's been a few years since I thought about high school like that and I did miss watching Wishbone on Fridays. I walk to my Mr. Cordova's desk and the only thing sitting on top is his funeral portrait in a neat frame and a written script at the bottom that says:

Jonathan Cordova
December 11, 1948 – February 22, 1994
My Dream Come True

You know how I told you your dream body goes on a mind ride? That it just goes along? Well this is different. I picked up the photo frame and felt like I was actually holding it in my hands. I could feel the texture of the mahogany wood beneath my fingers, and when I titled the glass at the right angle it caught the moonlight and reflected in my eyes and I had to blink from the sudden brightness. I just knew that this wasn't a dream, that it was something...different.

I put the frame down carefully and backed away. I didn't want to go back into the hallway anymore. I had the strange intuition that something was waiting for me there. So, I went to my old desk next to the window and looked outside, trying to distract myself until it was time to wake up because I had this sudden sense of dread and I couldn't figure out why or what to do to stop it.

Outside, I could see the courtyard immediately below and if I craned my neck slightly, I could even see the entrances to the cafeteria in the bottom left corner. But my sweet spot, the place where I would casually look out without contorting my head or shoulders in some weird way, was the school track, the one with the soccer field etched inside it to save the school district some money.

I looked outside there now, seeing as the night was interrupted there by a bright stadium light someone must have left on by accident before going home for the day.

Again, wasting money.

At first I didn't see anything remarkable, not until I noticed figures moving in the dark just outside the spotlight. I don't know what they were doing, they were just moving. Dancing? Fighting? Both? I couldn't tell you, but they were doing something.

I sat up straighter and pushed my head to the glass, trying to see if that would help me figure out who was out there. Then a second thought crossed my mind almost immediately: do I want to know?

Was it better to pretend that I never saw anything and hide under the desk until my real body woke up?

Whatever it was must have known it was being watched, because it stopped moving. Just stopped.

I thought that was it, the end of the show, but then one of the figures stepped forward slowly. I'm talking baby steps into the spotlight.

It was Sara.

And even from my desk hundreds of yards away, past the track, through the courtyard, past the school building and all the way to

Mr. Cordova's English 401 class, I could tell she smirked.

That same smirk.

And behind her?

Oh, no. I'm not there yet.

Yes, yes, I'm here because I'm talking right?

Look, I just feel all jumpy and nervous, could I get a cigarette? I swear I won't say shit, you can blame it on me, say I was acting crazy or something.

Thanks, buddy.

And a light?

They took mine when I came in here.

I know, it was a nice one, too, with my name engraved on the side and a black case all around.

Thanks.

You know, it's been thirteen years since I spoke about Sara.

And thirteen years since I had my last smoke.

Yeah, yeah. I'll cut to the chase.

So, in my dream. Right behind Sara was, well, it was Tessa.

All red hair and braces still like she'd never aged since the last time I saw her in class before she moved. Except this time she was lying face up in the grass and Sara had to pull her into the spotlight, like she was showing her off to me.

I feel sick thinking about it.

I felt sick seeing it.

But Tessa wasn't moving, and there's no way she'd sleep through being dragged like that across a soccer field. She was there, b-but she wasn't.

I squeezed my eyes shut, hoping that I would wake up from this awful dream and that everything would be normal when I did, but someone how it got worse.

I opened my eyes after counting to ten and Sara was still there, this time by herself under the spotlight.

She lifted her hand and waved. She waved excitedly like we'd been best pals and found each other at the mall or something. I mean, what the fuck was that.

Do you have an ashtray or do you want me to just tap it here on the table?

Okay, thanks, buddy.

Where was I?

Oh, yeah. So I finally wake up and I'm just soaked, truly buckets of sweat, and there may have even been a little piss. I can't tell because I'm drenched and frankly, I'm scared out of my goddamn mind. It's not every day you'll have a dream like that where you wake up wanting to hug your mom, but there we were.

I told Greg I wasn't working any more night shifts, and even though he threatened to fire me, he let me take the morning shifts with Deb and Juan. They were a pretty nice couple who were about a year older than me and were trying to keep busy in the summer, too.

They were the best part of that summer, if I'm being honest, and me and Juan even got into a little scuffle over who Deb would choose when we were drunk one Saturday night like the dumb kids we were.

Who won?

Well, I'll tell you. Deb and Juan ended up getting married a decade or so ago in Monterey because she liked the beaches out there and Juan just wanted to see her happy. It was a good wedding. I was one of the guests and had brought my ex-wife, since that's when things were still going good between us.

After that dream, I made sure to not be at the burger joint by myself anymore. It wasn't that I was scared of Sara, exactly, it was more that I was scared of what I didn't know about her. And I didn't think I wanted to find out. I tried to tell myself it was a silly dream and that Sara had gotten under my skin because she stared at me with those eyes and that damn smirk and it was a late night and I was high when it happened.

But every excuse under the sun couldn't explain what happened next.

Greg had given my closing shifts to a kid named Chris who started the next day. Guess he was strapped for cash and trying to pick up whatever the boss could give him. Chris just worked, played, and went to the beach about an hour or so away. The kid enjoyed living like a rock. Just there to be there.

After a couple of days, Chris says he's not feeling good. Has an upset stomach and had to call out. Apparently, according to Deb, another college student, Gina, who was working slow shifts decided to volunteer for Chris's shifts. It was only supposed to be for a day or two until Chris got better, but wouldn't you know, he's sick again his first day back. And then Gina gets sick with the flu.

Greg was having a panic attack. He thought it might've been something with the food, or maybe it was the ice cream machine, or maybe it was that employees weren't washing their hands as instructed after they used the restroom.

It was madness for the evening shift. Someone volunteers for Chris's shift, he comes back, gets sick, the volunteer gets sick, and again and again it's the same.

Luckily, I was on morning shift slugging out breakfast burgers and hashbrowns during the busier parts of the week, so I didn't get to see all that drama unfold. Me and Deb and Juan just did our thing, hung out after work and had a good time. And all the while, Greg's Burger Joint was an evening madhouse.

I didn't see Sara again that summer.

I was hoping I wouldn't ever see her again.

Not at the burger joint, not out and about, and especially not in my dreams.

I swear, I didn't think I'd ever go back to cigarettes so soon. My doctor told me my lungs were some of the healthiest he'd ever seen at my last checkup.

Yours did, too?

Something about these doctors, they know how to make you feel special.

Where was I?

Oh, yeah.

The next summer after my junior year of college, I headed back to the burger joint ready to ask for my old job back when the lady behind the cash register—I think her name was Sierra or Jasmine—tells me that Greg had died last fall.

"Greg? He looked fine when I saw him. What happened?" I asked her.

"He had a nasty illness that came out of nowhere. He fought for a few weeks before it finally took him. Not sure what it was, but I think I heard someone around here say his appendix burst and he took too long to get checked. I'm not sure, though."

I ask her about the other employees from last year and she has no clue who I'm talking about. Besides, the new manager seemed like an ass, so I decided to apply at the video rental store. There's just something about a videotape or DVD you can hold in your hands and have ready to watch on a moment's notice. I always liked the vibe of these places, and whenever I was bored, I would rewind tapes and watch the movies backwards and that was kind of a head trip, especially if you were a little high.

Anyway, the manager Trent was a cool guy, could talk your ear off for hours about any movie around. Some people find their calling sooner than others, I suppose. The girl I worked with was Alyssa and sometimes we would hook up in the back when no one was in the store just for the fun of it. I haven't talked to her since that summer. I did see her years later on a plane in Denver, but honestly, I wasn't sure so I didn't say hi.

That summer was starting off well, except of course for Greg's death, may he also rest in peace.

I was working late, rewinding tapes in the back when I heard the bell ding at the front. I didn't remember anyone coming in, so I figured I'd just dozed off since I was having trouble sleeping and walked to greet the customer.

Imagine my surprise when I see Sara fucking Diaz. Everything about her is the same as when I last saw her at the burger joint. Long hair, crazy brown eyes, a smirk like she's laughing at your expense.

"Sara. Hi? Can I help you?"

She loses the signature smirk and then it's back to those eyes, just staring through me from across the checkout counter.

"Um, we're going to be closing soon. Do you have a movie you want to rent?"

"Have your dreams come true?"

I just about lost it on the girl. I ask her why she keeps asking me that. I don't even realize I'm in tears—me, a grown twenty-one-year-old kid, crying in front of the weird girl from high school.

No, I didn't hit her or anything, just in case you wonder as you're taking these notes.

You didn't think so.

Okay, so…

I'm losing it and she just looks disappointed. I can't explain why this hits a nerve, I don't know why this bothers me so much, but it does. Then out comes Trent, and she freezes like a deer in headlights. For a moment, it's like she thinks she can stand still and be invisible. But then Trent says hi, sees my face and starts asking questions.

Can I bum another cigarette? It'll be my last one, I swear.

Thanks again.

So, she leaves. Same way as last time, running out as if she stole the whole joint even though she had nothing in her hands, not even a wallet. She runs into the parking lot and then turns right before a mechanic shop.

Then again, she's gone.

I hate these damn things, but just thinking about Sara makes me want to smoke a whole pack of them. It's what she does to you. Or rather...

Now, Mr. Greg from the burger joint.

I didn't know much about him, unfortunately other than he owned the place. He kept to the back office whenever I was on shift, unless I was closing and then he was at home having dinner with the wife and kids. He never seemed to like small talk much either. The man was a type A control freak—explains the meltdown over the illnesses.

But he paid me decent, accommodated me when I needed that switcheroo from the closing shift, and didn't bother me much. So, he gets a free pass.

Why am I telling you this?

I told you, patience.

I went home that night from the video store and just wanted to take a load off. I called up Alyssa and we hooked up at my place. After maybe an hour she had to head out, so I was alone again.

Like I said, I hate silence.

I flipped through the channels and I can't remember what I ended up watching because I fell asleep shortly after.

This time, I dreamed I walked inside the burger joint. The bell jingled at the top of the door and closed shut behind me. The smell of grease and milkshakes filled the air, but it was dark, far past closing as the only thing giving this place any light was the moon outside and that only worked because the windows spanned across most of the outside walls.

I didn't know what I was supposed to do, which was an odd thing to think about when you're dreaming, because you're supposed to let your dream body do the floating through while your mind experiences the ride. Or vice versa, whatever it says in your notes is what we'll go with.

I'm sorry, I'm exhausted.

Let me get my mind straight here.

Oh, yes. So, I walk into the burger joint and it's dark and dreamlike. Everything has that foggy quality and I'm just trying to figure out what I need to do to occupy my time before I have to wake up. Because in any dream you want to wake up, right?

Isn't there a study about if you die in your sleep you die in real life?

Maybe?

Yeah, I'll have to look that up later.

The burger joint isn't really a big place; you can walk around the whole inside of the diner in about a minute, two minutes if you include the kitchens and back office. So that's what I do, I wander. Because that's what we're supposed to do, wander.

Everything looks normal until I see that Mr. Greg's back office is slightly open. I've only ever been in there when I did my first interview and when I went to collect my check every Friday. I never thought much about it, if I'm being honest.

It had no windows, a basic brick wall, and a desk he kept the safes and ledgers behind.

But as I was wandering in my dream body, I walked to his office, expecting to see him in there for some reason or another because it never occurred to me until that moment that I had never seen the office without him in it.

I pushed open the door and everything was as it was, but there was no Mr. Greg inside. I remember I felt a bit upset. Like I said, I didn't know him well, but he wasn't a bad man. He had a wife and kids, I think I said. And he died so suddenly I didn't even hear about it while I was going to school.

A lamp flickered on the desk, revealing only a small slip of paper that lay on the otherwise bare desk. I could feel myself tense as I stared at it. I was curious, but also nervous. Why am I wandering into a dead man's office? Why am I asking such logical questions in a dream when I'm supposed to be going along for the ride?

I walked inside and looked at the paper.

It was my last paystub from the closing shift.

Nothing appeared off about it at all.

Then, I heard a tap. It was coming from outside the diner.

I'm so sorry, just one last cigarette, then I'm done I swear.

Thank you, so so much. I'm smoking them fast so I don't leave a mess or anything. Don't want the smoke detectors going off…

Okay, I'm ready.

I hear a tap like I'd hear during the morning shift when customers came before opening and would knock on the doors thinking they were the exception to the six o'clock opening rule.

I can still remember the feeling in my body, like I was no longer along for the ride, but that I was dipping into rollercoaster territory, plummeting down at superspeed into the earth. That exhilarating, terrifying sensation where you hope you'll make it out alive, but your body is rejecting hope and going for the feeling of the moment which is potential threat and danger.

Yes, that feeling, exactly.

That's what went through me then as I stepped out of the back office and moved past the kitchens into the main dining area.

But I froze the second I saw the front glass doors.

They were locked and on the other side was Sara.

She pressed her face and body against the glass, smirking as I stood only a few feet away. The doors and their thick glass seemed so fragile now, as if taking a single breath would make t crack and shatter as Sara was pressed against it.

She waved at me as she smirked.

That fucking wave. I can see it right now in front of me.

She pointed out into the parking lot, but I couldn't see more than a foot behind her. She must have sensed my confusion, because she lifted her finger, mouthed the word wait, and took off into the darkness.

The second she was out of my sight, my brain went into overdrive. I swear it was like a spell that wore off the second she was gone. I sprinted to the doors and made double sure they were locked. They were. No sooner had I done that than I looked up to see Sara dragging something into the moonlight.

She struggled a bit against it, but beamed with pride as her eyes met mine. Those dark brown eyes with secrets in them. She was acting just like she had in high school.

She waved again and dropped something from her hand as she did. I could hear it thump against the sidewalk and I knew, I didn't even look yet and I knew exactly what—or rather who—it was.

The leg thumped against the sidewalk, bounced barely a half inch back up, then stayed down. Sara grabbed it from the floor and continued to pull with me watching in utter horror as Mr. Greg was dragged before the glass door.

His stomach was in shreds, his eyes bulged out and looked in different directions. This was not the man I knew in life, but a dead one whose body was torn to pieces and left to be dragged by this girl who talked to air and pretended to read books.

I think the ash tray needs to be changed out. I don't wanna mess up your nice table here.

I know it gets messy because of all the interrogations, but I'd rather not be part of the mess. It might not seem like it—you know, as the young kid who smoked dope and had fucked up dreams about a girl from high school who kept in touch over the years in her own sick way—but I like some structure. I like things to be clean and orderly. I can handle that.

Thanks. This cigarette's almost out anyway, but if I'm already breaking my streak, I might as well make it worth it.

What happened?

Oh, I woke up.

I woke up and went to work at the video store. This time, I talked to my boss Trent about it, and he said it reminded him of a movie he watched once that he couldn't remember the name of but would get back to me on.

That was a first.

And he never did get back to me on that movie.

I don't know what I expected, really.

I didn't want to be there anymore, but summer was almost over and I had to get ready for my last year of college. I just hoped Sara wouldn't come back.

And she didn't.

And neither did Trent.

No reason given, but I was tapped as the interim manager for three days until the rental store owner sent down a woman from L.A. who was pretty down to earth and liked to talk about movies, too. So it wasn't too bad.

Me and Alyssa didn't see each other casually again after that night. Every time I saw her face, I wondered if she would be next on Sara's list. Because after two in a row, I was starting to think that Sara was making a list.

It sounds crazy, I know it does, but what was I supposed to think?

I wasn't safe in the day and I sure as hell wasn't safe when I slept. I went to one of those mind doctors, what are they called?

Ah, yes, psychiatrists.

Dr. Jerome Baker up in San Jose, because my dad used to work with him in the hospital and swore he was a great guy.

What did my parents think of this?

It sounds dumb to say, but I didn't tell them.

They just thought I was having a hard time and were doing their best. I didn't want to worry them with talk about a girl who stalked my dreams and dropped the bodies of dead people at my feet like a cat would a bird or a dog would a squirrel.

It was disturbing.

And I know I'm trying to keep my cool now, but I was losing it then. I couldn't tell whether I was asleep or awake sometimes. I would question everyone around me. I drove away some of my friends, started talking to myself, trying to convince myself that I wasn't in a dream. I couldn't have been in a dream. I wasn't an idiot, I knew people looked at me weird, especially in college where I would sit by the campus tree and people watch as I mumbled, trying to tell myself that if I was in a dream then he wouldn't do that and she wouldn't be able to say that.

I started carrying a book around so I could pretend that I was talking about the book I was reading. This was before cell phones were common, so it wasn't like I could pretend I was on a video call or anything like that.

No, just pure descent into madness with some '90s flair and spiked tips when I tried to act like one of the Backstreet Boys for a semester.

I'm rambling again, I apologize.

It's just that there are so many thoughts in my head and I feel like I can't get them out of my mouth quick enough so they trample over each other, and I'm sitting here hoping you understand what I'm saying.

It's dark, it's twisted. I'm making myself sick just thinking about it all.

I just wanted to be nice to the weird girl and ask her why she talked to the air and pretended to read books, and somehow that led to being cursed with her following me over thirty years of sleepless nights and dreams that make me want to gouge my eyes out. But I guess that wouldn't help because I still have memories of things I've seen and those things terrify me, but without new material perhaps I would just grow used to seeing Tessa on the track and Mr. Greg on the sidewalk outside of the burger joint.

But I guess we'll never know because my doctor also says I have perfect vision and that even in my middle age I still don't need glasses, so that's good to hear.

The rest of the nineties were a blur and so were most of the 2000s. I graduated and moved here to San Diego, I got married and divorced.

And no, I didn't have any kids.

Don't be sorry—I didn't want them. I didn't want to think about what Sara would do to torment them or me if she ever found out.

But I did have a dog, Button, who died about five years ago. That was rough. She definitely got me through the roughest patches of my life. I spread her ashes out toward the Pacific because she loved to go to the beach and bury her head in the sand and search for crabs and whatever other critters buried themselves in there.

She was fun.

Now?

No, I haven't got a new dog. I've been thinking about a cat, though. I'm still on the fence about it. Corporate grind is busy work for little pay, and I couldn't imagine leaving any animal alone at home for so long.

Retirement?

Hopefully one day. We'll see about that.

Sara?

Yes. And no. All in all I didn't see Sara again out and about. I think the best remedy for that was getting the hell out of that place and moving. Then when I got a cellphone, I only called my closest friends and family. I didn't use it all too much until this past decade where it seems like everything about our lives can be found on these devices.

Sara.

I would still see her in my dreams, lurking about and beckoning me to her. I'm not sure why, but we were always separated by something. A glass door, the school building, something.

I like to think it was my proof that I had not let her in my psyche completely, that I had some control over how she saw me and what she could do.

Sometimes, I would have those same dreams where Tessa's lying on the grass and I just turn away. I play tic-tac-toe on Mr. Cordova's chalkboard, I make myself some fries in the burger joint, I wander. Just wander.

Other times she gets really angry and pounds her fists against the glass window or screeches so loud I'm afraid it'll break the classroom windows. But it never does, and it still scares me.

I would lie awake next to my ex-wife at night watching how soundly and peacefully she slept. She would tell me about her dreams sometimes when she would get up in the morning, telling me about adventures in South America, eating her way through Italy, dancing at a bar in Tokyo.

I guess I should have taken the hint, but I was so busy trying to keep myself busy and distract myself from thoughts of Sara that I never once considered that I was losing out on someone who deserved more from me, more than a struggling dreamer who couldn't sleep more than a few hours, even with a bottle of the strongest sleeping pills the Dr. Baker could prescribe me.

In his professional opinion, my sleep distress was related to my real-life challenges and the best way to combat it was with a good night's sleep. He had a flair for sounding like a walking advertisement and I kind of liked that about him. He did conduct the usual tests, making sure I didn't have sleep apnea or other health concerns that could cause all these sleep issues, but my bill of health there was good. Nothing will make you feel more insane than a clean bill of health for a body that feels broken in ways you can't explain.

He was a good doctor, though. And he would listen as I told him about Sara and how she followed me around for all these years, about the deaths, about everything.

He would take copious notes, much like you're doing now, and claim that I wasn't crazy, because believe me, I've seen worse. I appreciated it when he said things like that. Whether or not it was true was another matter, and I never wanted to ask.

Bit by bit, I felt stronger each day because Dr. Baker said I was not crazy and that I was a healthy man. I needed to go out and live it.

The same day he told me that, I went to the florist, bought the biggest bouquet I could find for my wife and strutted home with her favorite chocolates, the kind with cherries on the inside in the heart shaped box. It wasn't even Valentine's, but I just felt good. You know, I just felt good.

I walked inside my home and there was my wife.

Standing there with mascara running down her cheeks, a ring on the table, and the paperwork she swore she told me she'd get months ago if I didn't get my act together.

She left to stay at a friend's house while the divorce was settled, and I let her take the flowers and chocolates. It was the least I could do for someone who spent nearly a decade dealing with my mess.

That word again. Didn't we use that earlier in this conversation?

I'm much better at keeping myself together nowadays.

Here's the ash tray, Bob.

Thank you for the cigarette, Derek.

I know we're not done yet, I just want to make sure I check all the boxes before I finish. I'm keeping my messes clean, literally and figuratively.

When's the next time I saw Sara in person?

Well, it's like I told your partner here, I saw her outside my office. I'm a glorified paper pusher at an accounting firm.

Yes, I know you know, but I just need to say it out loud or my brain will get all jumbled with the details.

So, paper pusher.

Accounting firm.

Ah, yes, so I usually work late there. I don't technically get paid any overtime due to a loophole the company uses to make bonuses count. It's a mess, but I work late because pushing paper is busy when everyone sends you tons of shit to push along and even more complicated if they want you to approve it all for the next higher review. I'm talking cost estimates, billing, bookkeeping, the works. Anything you want to go through accounting usually comes to me first.

I agree, it's incredibly inefficient, but no one wants to hear an old man's ideas anymore. And I'm so close to retirement that I'd rather just sit and push paper and wait until I can leave that damn place and finally get a cat.

Yes, I've thought about it while I've been talking and I think I want to get a cat. They keep to themselves and I keep to my own. They'll make sure to keep the mice at bay and I'll make sure they're fed and have clean litter.

So, she's standing outside of my office and the only reason I know is because I have this urge to look out the window. I'm on the fourth floor and I can look down and see the parking lot from where I sit. It's a shitty view, but at least there's a window. So that's better than nothing.

I see her and immediately my blood runs cold and I get this awful feeling in my gut. That same I felt when I was a twenty-one-year-old kid seeing her pull Mr. Greg's body to the front door of the burger joint. It all starts coming back to me like a slap in the face or a punch in the gut, whatever the saying is.

I can't help it, I am utterly lost and confused. I look around and of course I'm alone, no one else works this late for shitty pay and no one else wants to spend their free time in a fourth-floor office building when they have families and lives to live.

It's only me.

My eyes are still good, if you remember, and so as I stare out the window down to her, feeling like the floor is being ripped out from under me, the oddest thought goes through my head.

What if this isn't Sara? What if this is some older woman who bears a resemblance to the woman who visits me in my dreams, who only looks like the girl from high school with a wild look in her eyes and a smirk that says she has secrets you will never uncover?

There's a single lamppost lighting the area around the parking lot she stands in, and we are not completely alone. Across the street there are businesses and a shopping center, the traffic there is moderately heavy and the lights of those areas reflect toward us.

Maybe this isn't Sara.

It could be anyone working in this ten-floor high rise who also wants to work late because her boss is a jerk that doesn't know how to pay well and scams the employees' overtime to make the books work in his favor.

Against my better judgement, I admit, I decided to see.

I pressed the button to the elevator, terrified that the doors would open to reveal Sara waiting inside for me with sharp fangs and a serpent's tongue. But when the bell dinged, it opened to no one as the sound of Billie Holiday played over the speakers. And of course, it's "I'll Be Seeing You," which immediately makes me think of The Notebook because my ex-wife made me watch it at least a hundred times and that scene where they dance in the street is romantic.

I should have taken her to dance in the street like that.

Sometimes I feel like we have the playbook right in our hands and we still fumble because we aren't actually paying attention. We just pretend we do and go about our days thinking that a semblance of effort is better than no effort at all, but really it just shows that we have it in us and choose to do the bare minimum. I don't know what's worse, but I'll leave that up to your opinion.

The elevator goes down and the music crescendos as the doors open to the first-floor lobby. We have a turnstile door that locks after eight P.M. and seeing as it's ten, I have to use the regular front push door.

I don't open it, though. Not yet.

I need to see if this is really her, if this is Sara in the flesh after three decades of torture and pain and heartache and loss. I need to see it with my own eyes.

I don't care if that doesn't make sense, I just needed to know. I had to know.

The woman looks like Sara.

She has the same brown hair, with hints of gray speckled in.

She has the same brown eyes that are giving me that strange look.

She has the same smirk that twitches slightly on the right side of her face.

"Can I help you?" I ask.

She presses against the door and pulls to open it. But it's locked to outsiders after eight, which means this is Sara and not a disgruntled employee who doesn't have anything else to do on a Friday night but

work overtime for a company that doesn't care to pay her well.

No.

This is Sara.

I swallow.

Now I feel that dread pricking just at the nape of my neck again.

My stomach is in knots.

I feel queasy.

I feel sick.

She just looks at me and smiles.

It would be welcoming if she weren't my nightmares come to life before my eyes.

"Have your dreams come true?" she asks, fogging up the glass door.

The air looks thick outside.

The darkness now covers everything but whatever the light of the single lamppost touches.

She looks at me and her eyes meet mine, waiting for my answer.

"Have yours?" I ask. It's more of a whisper, I admit. I was surprised I was able to say anything at all, but somehow my little voice managed to make the sound and Sara narrowed her eyes.

"Have your dreams come true?!" She banged her hand against the door, repeating her words over and over again.

Have your dreams come true?!

Have your dreams come true?!

Have your dreams come true?!

It feels like the building is shaking, I can feel the earth rumbling beneath my feet. But I'm thinking, this can't be a dream, this can't be a dream. No, certainly, not, this cannot be a dream.

I did my checks like I do every morning, I even locked my door twice and walked around my bedroom once in a circle and twice in a square.

Look, it makes sense to me, okay?

That's not the point.

The building is on the verge of collapsing and I go to my knees, I'm screaming.

"Why won't you leave me alone?! Leave me alone!"

And then she stops. Her hand is bloodied and bruised, her face twists ever so slightly and she holds up a finger.

I know what she's about to do as she steps back into the darkness.

I know, deep in my gut I know what's about to happen.

I'm begging for anything out there, for it not to be my ex-wife, not any of the friends I've made and lost along the way, none of the people who are good and innocent and kind and…

She drags the body from the shadows and now my own face is pressed against the glass, watching with bated breath to see who it may be this time.

She grunts as she throws her body weight against the figure. It lands with a thud before me and I vomit on the lobby floor.

It's Trent, my old manager from the video rental store.

Sara smiles, positively beaming as she walks back to the door.

I'm too stunned to speak, too stunned to move my eyes from the corpse that is Trent. He has decayed horribly, the stench so strong even with the airsealed glass door between us. Tears fall down my cheeks. I am mad with fear and rage.

When will these deaths stop?!

When will she leave me alone?!

"Get out!" I bellow with the angriest voice I can manage.

Because I was angry. I am angry.

This senseless violence, these horrible, horrible deaths.

I—

I won't ever be able to not see it. I will never be able to walk through life again and not see their faces in my dreams.

She looked disappointed.

And I nearly lost it, stepping back to channel all the strength I had into pushing open the door when I felt two arms tighten around my midsection, holding me back.

It was Frank, the security guard. Apparently, he took a piss break and came back to see me vomiting and raging at the woman on the other side of the door. He told me he thought I was going to damage company property, but I can assure you that I am not in the mood to push that kind of paperwork.

So no, no company property harmed except the puke I cleaned up. But that's fixed now.

Sara?

She did what she always did.

She ran, like she always did, to the parking lot, not looking both ways, not paying attention when the Chevy hit her. The kids thought the parking lot was empty and thought they'd learn how to drift like they saw on TV. It's not their fault—they're kids, and she was the one who went like a bat out of hell. Though, I'm sure you all will review the footage.

Can you let me know if you see Trent on it, too?

I just want to see something.

Thank you, I really appreciate that.

I wish I could say I was the hero who sprang into action, but I was dumbstruck and numb. It was like watching it happen in terrifying slow motion, the way her body collided with the car and flew back into the asphalt.

I called you guys hoping she would make it out alive.

I wanted her to stop tormenting me, but I didn't want her to die.

I just wanted her to stay out of my head and away from my dreams because she was driving me mad.

I can't even remember the last time I got a decent night's sleep where she or the-the-the bodies weren't haunting me.

I can still see that smirk when I close my eyes, the way she would give me that disappointed fucking look as if I had let her down on some promise I don't ever remember making!

I-I'm sorry, I don't mean to cry.

I'm just…I just don't know what this means.

Am I free or am I a prisoner?

No.

No, that question wasn't for you two. It was for her.

I'm just talking out loud because I ramble a lot. And all these questions are like pistons in my head firing again and again and again.

Like, am I going to go home tonight and get the first peaceful night's sleep I've had since '95?

Do her victims actually rest in peace?

Am I finally free of her?

Or have my dreams come true?

AUTHOR'S NOTE

Good evening, dear reader,

I assume it is evening where you are because it is the middle of the night where I am and it would be odd at this hour to say something like good morning or happy Monday, which it technically is, but that's all besides the point.

Here in my home where it is a little past the midnight hour, I am writing this author's note and checking my I's and dotting my T's before sending this manuscript to my editor to be…well, edited.

And seeing as though you are finishing my collection of stories, I wanted to chat a bit, if you will, about the madness behind the madness, to give you a little peek behind the curtain about how this collection of horror stories came to be.

It is no secret that the word "horror" alone can provoke feelings of fear or excitement (and perhaps, even both). Horror can include ghosts, demons, vampires, folklore, or plain reality that keeps you up at night trying not to think about the places your imagination will go.

It's the beauty of reading strange and daunting literature. Your subconscious will pick up on the phrase or story that makes the wheels in your mind turn ever so slightly, and soon you will find yourself remembering the feeling years down the road after you've sworn off all things scary. And most of the time you'll think about it as you are tucked in, ready for bed with the lights turned off, wondering if that shadow in the corner is really a shadow or something far more sinister.

You may be scared and hide under your covers or you may flick on the switch and realize it's just the lamp and have a good laugh. But at some point, you fall asleep.

Because it was just your imagination, remember?

Each story in this collection was made up of decades worth of scribblings and fervent typing sessions after a bout of nightmare-induced insomniatic episodes. Since childhood, I had intense sleep paralysis and from it came the most bizarre and horrifying imaginings. For years, I kept these stories stuffed in a drawer or on the computer, waiting for the moments when I would feel most inclined to reach for them. But every time I walked past the drawer or flipped through the folders of unfinished works on my laptop, I felt that strange chill, my hands would become clammy, and I would be reminded of the places my mind would take me as I tried to sleep.

As I finished my other novels and prepared my next publishing schedule, I realized I had enough room to release a collection of stories. I once again browsed through my files, thinking I would subvert genre-expectations and go for something unpredictable. I wrote and rewrote numerous other stories from romance to non-fiction to literary fiction, but nothing felt quite right in the moment.

I was sitting at the library one day staring at the mocking cursor blinking over and over again (as it most often does when I am experiencing incredible writer's block). Frustrated, I put on my headphones and set my playlist to shuffle. The soundtrack for The Haunting of Hill House began playing—it seems I forgot to remove it from when I was writing Flame in the Silver

Storm months back.

But that's a story for another day. Anyway, those ominous tones and haunting melodies did the trick.

Words tumbled out of me nearly faster than my fingers could type and before I knew it, I had finished "Forty Minutes," the story of a woman driving home in the desert, letting herself become overwhelmed by her foreboding imagination.

A slow, quiet horror that built into something quite dreadful. The theme fell into place shortly after, stories based around the horrors of our imaginations.

More specifically, the way our heads will play tricks and convince us that there is indeed something in the closet, or under the bed, or within the dark corner even though we've checked a dozen times already. And it's the painstaking millisecond before you check these places with a bat in your shaking hand that your mind conjures the most horrific and frightening things awaiting you.

It's a universal and visceral feeling.

I realized then that I needed to dust off the pages in the drawer and open the files on my desktop. It was time to confront the horrors that plagued the innermost part of my psyche.

Because the truth is that it's all in our heads, isn't it?

That's where the real horror begins.

With love & dread,

Rocio

ACKNOWLEDGMENTS

A dream is nothing without a team to make it a reality. Thank you first and foremost to my phenomenal editor Meg, who took such great care with this work. You were always at the top of my list for horror editors and having you on board to review this passion of mine meant the absolute world.

Thank you to my family, who without their support, I would still be dreaming away instead of making it happen. I couldn't imagine living this amazing life without you.

And finally, thank you to you, dear reader.

If not for you reading my work, these pages would simply be diary entries that may have never seen the light of day. Your endless support means so much to me.

Here's to many more stories to come…

ABOUT THE AUTHOR

ROCIO CARRANZA is the author of this and several other works, including *Blood of the Blackthorn, Flame in the Silver Storm, Lana Lang,* and *Miss Reliable.* Forever a dreamer and creative, Rocio spends her free time building worlds on paper and film that may never see the light of day, but spark joy in her soul. She lives with the ever-jovial Allen and their two sons in Austin, TX. *My Dreams Come True* is her first story collection.

VISIT THE AUTHOR ONLINE:
www.rociocarranza.com

INSTAGRAM & THREADS:
@rociocarranzawrites

TIKTOK
@rociocarranzawrites

www.ingramcontent.com/pod-product-compliance
Lightning Source LLC
Chambersburg PA
CBHW050323110726
47899CB00007B/2352